THE BELLS OF AUTUMN

THE BELLS OF AUTUMN

A NOVEL

JAMES HUFFERD

SUNSTONE
PRESS

SANTA FE

Sunstone books may be purchased for educational, business, or sales promotional use.
For information please write: Special Markets Department, Sunstone Press,
P.O. Box 2321, Santa Fe, New Mexico 87504-2321.

Book and cover design › Vicki Ahl
Body typeface › Minion Pro
Printed on acid-free paper
∞
eBook 978-1-61139-305-7

Library of Congress Cataloging-in-Publication Data
Hufferd, James.
  The Bells of Autumn : a novel / by James Hufferd.
    pages cm
  ISBN 978-1-63293-017-0 (softcover : alk. paper)
  1. Wyoming--History--Fiction. 2. Whites--Relations with Indians--Fiction.
  3. Fathers and sons--Fiction. 4. Historical fiction. I. Title.
  PS3608.U3499B45 2014
  813'.6--dc23
                              2014024585

WWW.SUNSTONEPRESS.COM
SUNSTONE PRESS / POST OFFICE BOX 2321 / SANTA FE, NM 87504-2321 /USA
(505) 988-4418 / ORDERS ONLY (800) 243-5644 / FAX (505) 988-1025

Fiction is, it's said, a pack of lies: So be it! But I have opted for what I'm calling Enduring Truth, in one sense surpassing the tried and tested Documentary kind with its open wounds. Though not all here is strictly documentable, I have enlivened the unknowable spaces that always separate speculation from reality, and no doubt have exposed thereby interesting plausibilities.

—James Hufferd

CONTENTS

PART I ▷ WINTER

1

DANIEL EDGEMONT

The nonstop snows of December transfered custody to the dry-socket cold moan of January. Christmas's bright greens and reds were swept away by the gritty, chilling wind clawing down the Northern Plains as 1902 gave way to 1903. Ensconced in the drafty dugout shared with his Pa, a man known as Old Chessler, young Daniel Edgemont pulled his bulky buffalo robe forward to cover his ears and gnawed the last shred, nibbled as a sort of farewell, from his yearly New Year's Day turkey drumstick. He thought, as he sometimes did, of the irony of wearing for warmth the hide of an animal species he'd never been privileged to see, lest it was when he was two or three—he dimly recalled a hunched-shouldered calf that had wandered into their brown autumn yard in Field City, a town that no longer existed. But even that might have been a calf of the more usual sort.

Old Chessler came in huffing and exhaling white frost, toting a heavy log from out on the edge of the escarpment over the creek. He gave it a heave-ho, and ashes and sparks filled the close quarters. "We could use a bucket o' water when ya git around, and go down an' check for eggs, too, if ya would," he said to Daniel.

"Okay, I will do it," the boy answered slowly and dreamily, pulling his mind back into his body as he stirred himself. With a hearty lurch, he rose like a Christmas morning Jack-in-the-box from the low bench of the table and tripped toward the heavy door.

The door, hewn of logs, was all but stuck shut by the wind and had to be shouldered open. The cold on the other side pierced Daniel's sparse leggings, giving him the illusion of no shoes at all.

Daniel Edgemont was born on April 12, 1889, in a little town over in South Dakota, so he was told, and brought as a dark-eyed babe of a few months back to Weston County, on the Wyoming side of the remote state line, after Chessler and another man passing through the neighborhood retrieved him from a burned-out cabin where his mother, an abandoned lady named Mrs. Preston, had died of inhaled smoke. Daniel and Chessler, who was already 50 and what an Aussie shepherd he once met would have called an "old *cove*," took to each other fine, and Daniel had had a good upbringing, though far from rich. Their poverty mattered little to Daniel: he knew he couldn't have landed with a better soul for a pa.

When Daniel was little, the only thing that had bothered him was not having a mama. He thought that he could remember having a mama once—though there's no way he could have—and thought hard and seriously about that problem for someone so young.

A couple of times, he could barely remember now, his Pa had brought a woman in for a day or two. But though he heard lots of laughter through the closed door of the other sleeping room in the night, the woman was not a real mama and avoided looking at curious little Daniel, and never, ever came back a third time. And the other thing he remembered was old Chessler's deep sighing afterward, seemingly as disappointed and mystified as the boy.

Daniel grew up to be handsome, dark and fine-featured, with black, wavy hair. He was taller than most of the boys his age, of narrow shoulders and small bone structure, but he was lithe and quick, and could perhaps have been athletic if given the chance. Neat, clean and pleasant, and generous with his smiles, it was known and grudgingly admitted throughout Newcastle that he was, hands down, the brightest boy at the school, that big, lonely cathedral of education up a hundred steps at the top of the hill overlooking the town. And his one true school friend, Penny Osgood, was the smartest girl at the school.

But despite his abundant good qualities, Daniel was largely—almost inexplicably—steered clear of by his schoolmates. Assuredly, not everyone his age could have voiced the underlying reason for his shunning. But the leaders knew, and only Penny possessed the gumption and courage to pretend not to notice—for which Daniel was eternally grateful.

He remembered having playmates when he was little, girls and boys from the neighborhood, both before and after they moved from Field City to Newcastle. But except for Penny, all of them seemed to pull away at about the time he turned twelve, as Pa, with his help, cut a whole series of loads of lumber a ways north to sell to incoming house-builders.

The way Daniel's schoolmates acted toward him reflected the way their elders talked and acted. Few ever spoke to Daniel, just as few adults addressed Chessler to his face. The open hospitality and rousing fellowship considered so characteristic of the West was held in abeyance in their case, as if they were conspicuously different in some respect. Only the very lowly, and strangers to the town, ever came anywhere close to their door out beyond the tracks and shacks, while the townsfolk rarely gave Daniel or Old Chessler more than a perfunctory nod of recognition. But they were left at liberty and not harassed, as long as they kept to themselves and did not push any point.

In 1903, Daniel was just beginning to understand, or perhaps accept, that the reason they were shunned had something to do with his Pa—to him, the best man in the whole world. For reasons he couldn't begin to fathom, his Pa had been banished from society by Martin, the town's powerful and apparently heartless benefactor. He knew the reason his Pa didn't strike back had to do with him—his Pa wouldn't even take a chance of putting Daniel in danger. Tears at times welled up in Daniel's eyes and his heart literally ached at the strangeness and seeming finality of it.

But he loved his town, Newcastle, and Weston County just as fiercely, and his pointer dog Red and the pine- and sage-clad hills and minor peaks and grassy stream bottoms, endless series of plateaus, and even the little drafty clay-floored dugout, more a home from the pioneer days than the twentieth century. It wasn't much, but it was theirs, and he wouldn't have left it all for the world.

Unbeknownst to Daniel, his Pa had been warned anonymously that if he tried to build more of a house for himself than the lone surviving pioneer dugout out beyond the west end of Spruce Street, he could count on it being burned down immediately.

◄►

Daniel and Penny, sitting in desks side by side up in the eighth-year room, talked and laughed about everything but their home life. Though he'd never seen Martin come to the school, Daniel realized that Penny was indeed the granddaughter of the most feared and revered man in the county, the old man in the dun western hat he had only seen once or twice from the edge of a crowd, but heard spoken of almost daily on everybody's lips, as in "Martin wants this," "Martin wants that."

Daniel had seen "Young Martin" (more often called "Manfred"), Penny's odd, doltish father, pick her up at the plateau stop below the school ground in a fancy-looking two-horse phaeton. But she never spoke of her family, and he never mentioned old Chessler or his dog Red, and neither of the friends ever asked the other about anything at home. Those were the ground rules.

But at the big, crowded room at school, the only place they ever saw each other, everything and everybody else was fair game and enjoyed immensely and endlessly. If anyone else so much as whispered, they were called down and, not infrequently, rapped on the knuckles. But never Penny or, by extension, her friend Daniel. For, no teacher, nor certainly the callow and at times cruel students, would ever dare take on Martin's spawn. So Daniel had practically his whole social life away from the primitive dugout in that one, glorious extended conversation, with that one, single finest of U.S. Wyoming girls there ever was. Life was good!

The other thing Daniel had, his one extravagance, was a John Kemp Stanley bicycle. Far from new now, Chessler had gotten it for him someplace, and he rode it with a certain amount of freedom around the mining roads and hill tracks surrounding the town, when practically no one else had one. Chessler warned him to steer clear of riding it down the streets of the town, lest jealousy and animosity should strike. But the freedom was his, under those mild and reasonable conditions.

And when not at school or riding his bike, Daniel spent his time with his Pa, Old Chessler. As a veritable outcast, Chessler was restricted to doing custodial tasks for the town. He rang the church bells on Sundays and special occasions. He periodically ran the honey wagon for the part of town not yet on the sewer. He served as a courier when called upon. And, when he could get away, he ran a water business at a spring next to the old stage road east of town, scarce traveled now.

Lately, the man and his boy spent increasing time together out at the water springs station.

Out there at the well, they occupied an old shell of a cabin hidden down in a low place that no one else paid mind to, or possibly even knew about. They regularly cultivated a small garden there in summer as well, hauling water to irrigate it in buckets until, finally, enough pipe segments—eschewing totally lead-content ones—had been salvaged from here and there and cobbled together adequately to move water downhill from barrels suspended with a pulley above the spring. Actual water sales to travelers were rare, especially since, with the rail line passing nearby, most of the traffic on the road now consisted of indigents, who were provided life-sustaining draughts free.

Indeed, Chessler could only be out there when relatively certain he wouldn't be demanded elsewhere. But there was more allure than people knew.

In mid-afternoon of January 1, 1903, with the mercury standing at the day's high of 12 degrees, Daniel and Chessler loaded up their buckboard with ropes and gear and harnessed Jerry and Lanie. With Red aboard, they headed over the jouncing, now snow-packed trail around the south rim of Newcastle, past Highland Street, over to the old wreck of a cabin hidden down in the hole just up the old stage road from the flowing well.

Once there, Daniel, feeling the savage wind blow through, hunkered down in his buffalo coat and waited inside the walls. He watched his Pa through the paneless south window, shivering in the cold. Chessler lowered himself down into the cleft, the nearest point where the trace ran along the rim of the boulder-filled minor canyon. The boy kept an eye on him steadily for half an hour at least, until a familiar carriage pulled by a team of unusual-looking ghost-gray horses appeared, coming from the south. The driver, a friend from times past and farther south, well-paid, dismounted and, with much effort, took on board a small but exceedingly heavy parcel covered with canvas. The horses were then directed to wheel around, and disappeared back in the direction from which they had come.

The deed done, Daniel readied the buckboard. Chessler joined him, and with Red down between them, Daniel drove them back around, facing the last weak rays of sun, to share deep nighttime silence in the fire-lit dugout.

2

OLD CHESSLER

Chessler drifted into Weston County, still then the southern part of Crook County, in 1884 or '85, working as a teamster and horse wrangler with no settled address. On only a few occasions, he later related to his adopted son Daniel precious tidbits from his earlier life.

Old Chessler was born at the end of March 1846 in the upper Mississippi Valley near Cassville, Wisconsin. On which side of the river, and in which jurisdiction, he didn't say, and maybe didn't know. His pa, Edward Chessler, had been an iron and hardware man, and when they followed the frontier west in the 1850s, his ma, Mabel Ann, had her heart set on Oregon so kept right on going, on the arm of the wagon master, out of their lives forever. Edward Chessler applied for the open position of sutler at Fort Laramie, the halfway house of western emigration and all remunerative activities, in the uplands on the north fork of the Platte in what was then the westernmost edge of Nebraska Territory.

The sutler post had been vacated when the prior holder of it, a scowling youthful version of the same Martin who was in later years the tyrant of Weston County and Newcastle, was dismissed for selling the Indians whiskey—some said *poisoned* whiskey—and guns. It was rumored that Martin's aim was to provide the Indians with enough liquor and guns that they'd shoot each other, thus ridding the country of the scourge of the red-skinned savage. Martin, whose mother was shot with an arrow through the head by a band of Sioux one day before their arrival at the fort, had never forgiven the Indians that singular great crime. Now succeeded at his lucrative post by an Indian-lover, Martin, embittered and silent, put out bids for hauling between all of the far-flung forts and bided his time until he could exact revenge.

The wide new world was full of fascination for a little tousle-headed boy living at an emigrant post. Most of young Chessler's playmates were the young Sioux and Cheyenne who showed up in tow at the post store, and before long, he was reasonably fluent in both languages and went out and stayed overnight at least a hundred times, and even traveled and went hunting with his new best friends.

He was schooled at Fort Laramie and knew and was known to all the powerful, good, and bad actors who pulled up a quadrangle chair or leaned on a counter or danced a schottische at the post week in and week out, year in and year out, to refresh, visit, restock, and let off steam. And he eyed the ever disgruntled, aloof rogue Martin as much as any of the others.

He was present as a boy of seven when a party of Sioux women gathering roots was pistol-whipped and their packhorse shot at close range by a pair of wayward covered-wagon men. A year or two later, he saw two non-offending Lakota men scouting for antelope shot by a buffalo hunter. And he was saved from drowning in a hole in a stream by an elder while swimming with young Cheyenne friends. Unknown to his pa, he learned his earliest lesson about sex at eight from Standing Rose, the prettiest and normally shiest little girl he ever saw in his life, whom he could likely have married one day had she not succumbed at 13 to the white man's smallpox. And he played once with the infant Jack Red Cloud, Chief Red Cloud's son, born in 1862, in the bustling quadrangle of Fort Laramie.

When a bit older, he marveled at how the dignified adult Indians, spiritually mature and serene, suffered with great patience the condescending visits of the white Presbyterian missionary couple, Edna June and Charles Baker. At least, that was his view, as they seemed to him to treat everyone, up to the most seasoned chiefs and braves as though they were either children or feeble-minded. Even so, the Lakota consistently treated them with the greatest respect as exemplifying the Great Spirit, although in some strange and unfathomable way. He even concluded at one point—until he eventually learned otherwise—that no other white understood Indians to the extent that he knew them, or really valued them very much at all.

When the Civil War began, every new arrival from the east had news, it seemed, almost none of it pleasant, but all of it awaited breathlessly in the posts. Chessler, Daniel's Pa, was too young to go at the outset of the struggle. Sure, he nursed his dreams, night and day, of somehow deepening his voice and acting older and wearing tall boots and a tall hat to try and bluff his way into recruitment down in Colorado, where his slightly older school chums were heading to sign up.

Suspecting as much, Edward Chessler had sat his son down one day and confessed that he, too, was tempted to go and enlist. But, he said, somehow convincingly, he felt that he and his son alike were doing something more valuable for the young nation here on the frontier than they would be by throwing their poor, weak bodies and limited energies into the fight. They were here to secure the nation's future, he said, as well as their own. And it was true! There was plenty for both of them to do, along with a crew of four young hired lads and a cooking and cleaning woman who became young Chessler's model of sane and reserved womanhood. All of them were involved together in stocking and running the store, keeping the head-smashing and gun-holery to a minimum, and, increasingly in the younger Chessler's case, frantically trying to explain the strange, different behavior and perspectives of the surrounding native part of the clientele to the drifters and drovers, emigrants, soldiers, and grifters who happened through in an endless rude and restless stream.

What was so hard about understanding that the Indians had their own perspectives and beliefs and ways, and were not in some way slow or stupid because they had not grown up in white society? And yet, often, he alone seemed to have picked that up—with the only occasional arrival on the scene of someone who nodded with simple understanding when he made the point in defense of his friends and tutors. His own father warned him repeatedly to "watch it" and not go overboard with that, because the Indians' presence on the Plains was bound not to last much past the current generation.

Young Chessler was shocked and made frantic by the breakdown of the 1851 Fort Laramie treaty and the start of violent hostilities along the road in 1864 between the Sioux and Cheyenne and the soldiers stationed in the forts. Were there not vast enough spaces—the whole wide West—that could be shared so that everyone could live just as they wished? Why could the Indians not be hired on the nearby ranches starting up or in the towns that were bound to arrive, if they wanted to be? And, if not, left with half the land and *their* cattle, the bison, completely at liberty and with a promise of security? Why was "extermination," the word on half the lips in the world?

Who, after all, he asked mainly himself, were the happier and more settled in their lives and daily affairs, anyway? Did he want to be an Indian? No. Then, how many of them would want to become a white man? Or to have their land stolen from under them, and die?

There was the war to free the Negroes, he guessed. And then, there was the war necessitated by un-neighborly treatment and selfishness to "exterminate" or at least dispossess the Indian. It was, he agreed with his disabused friends, a world gone mad.

But, what good would it do if he told every white man how he felt, and paid with his life, too? And neither could he go to the Indians, because not all of them knew or cared about him.

So, left to keep his silence and live his life according to convention, at 19 Chessler moved in with Alda Jackson, an older former schoolmate, over his Pa's heated objections. They had twins and lived in contentment until one night the Sioux attacked. The twins and Alda were killed, charred beyond recognition in the little log house in the brush near the post. Heartbroken, in shock, Chessler headed the next day to Fort Laramie and signed onto the rotation as a hauler.

At the end of the Sioux War, sometime in 1867, on a haul trip to Fort Fetterman he met two of his boyhood Indian friends on the road coming down to the Fort Laramie post. The ordeal of Alda and the babies was never raised, because he had recognized as the killers on the fateful night his boyhood tormenter, Runs-From-Crow, outcast from the Lakota along with the toadying moron Blue Bear, both themselves killed in subsequent senseless attacks. And so, the matter was not broached now with his friends, who had suffered their own losses and woes. He grieved and felt his loss more deeply than anything ever in his life, but was of strong fiber and wisely managed to hold it inside. He was fairly sure they'd had nothing to do with it, and two of them consoled him aside. And so it was that they remained friends as before. His pa, Edward, understood and forgave him as well.

Wyoming Territory was born out of vast Dacotah the very next year—in 1868.

Old Chessler remembered having written down in his chap book in 1869 or '70—that "While it is true, as commonly said, that general settlement cannot coexist in Wyoming with marauding Indians, there's a sort of accommodation that can be satisfied by appealing to reason and the good will of all." But, sadly, he reflected, that was a sentiment he hardly ever dared to voice beyond his own door. And the thought was general that the Indian probably was as doomed as their herds of buffalo.

Chessler continued hauling as a teamster working for the sutler at Fort Laramie for years and watched the raw, wide-open territory slowly grow and change as the cattle business began to implant and the military and native character of Wyoming north of its Union Pacific southern corridor began to give way to a cattle camp and military post culture, as the Indians were being elbowed out of their enormous hunting grounds and were, naturally, beginning to push back again.

◀▷

A development in the middle of the 1870s seemed to shove the inevitable along, as gold was discovered in the Black Hills of western Dacotah, sacred ground to the Sioux and promised to them as part of a vast permanent Sioux homeland to be protected from white encroachment. With the discovery of Black Hills gold, though, everything changed. Wealth seekers began at once to demand admittance to the Hills, flush up against the Wyoming Territory border; so close, in fact, that some were of the opinion that at least a major part of the gold fields must lie in Wyoming Territory itself.

Such proved not to be the case, but the repercussions of opening the Black Hills to the invaders certainly spilled quickly across, and to the Lakota Sioux, it meant a last stand and war.

Chessler was again made frantic by these ominous events. But he had no allies—none whatsoever—in arguing for fairness and consideration for the Indians, who were now commonly referred to as "fiends." So finding no alternative, he bit his tongue and lay low, keeping at his work.

Then, one day early in 1876, word passed among the civilians employed at Fort Laramie that a meeting was being called, out near the old Kingfisher post, to organize what was being called a "Wyoming Volunteer Regiment." The Regiment's objective was to protect the civilian citizens of the scattered cattle stations and small towns from surprise Indian attack by taking the offensive. Any of the civilian employees of the Fort who failed to attend the meeting would be noted and marked for reprisal. Edward Chessler's old nemesis Martin, weathered, usually laconic, and deathly serious, delivered the message to young Chessler in person on horseback, warning him, in no uncertain terms, that he dare not be a slacker.

When young Chessler reached the designated meeting site, just past noon on April 4, after reports of hostilities and army patrol skirmishes had already begun to filter in, he found a rag-tag looking cadre of teamsters, cooks, carpenters, and shelf-stockers, about a hundred, he guessed, milling around or hunched down on the grass of the river bank between the retreating snowdrifts. He greeted one or two of the men and lads he knew, and knelt down on the grass with a familiar group.

Then, almost at once, he was astounded to behold a rider with a broad black hat verily pop into their midst, and amazed to find that the man was none other than Martin. In a booming voice no one had ever heard before, Martin announced that he was henceforth to be addressed as "Colonel" and was himself the commander of the newly-formed "Wyoming Volunteer Regiment." Every man present was expected to sign the organizational charter, obligating them to a 100-day period of service in ridding the land of the "savage red man." To command attention and respect, he wielded as long and sharp a bullwhip as Chessler had ever beheld.

He assembled the men into small units of eight or ten each and had them stand at attention while he rode around from one to the next and assigned each to a specific duty.

To young Chessler's great surprise, he rode straight over to him and directed him to remove himself from the company of the men he knew and join a unit of seven near-total strangers under the command of a severe-looking colleague with a peculiar hooked nose named Simon. Martin ordered this unit to ride out toward the northeast the next morning, with instructions to "exterminate" a known encampment of Cheyenne and another nearby of Lakota.

When he had made the rounds to all the groups, this suddenly confident commander, "Colonel" Martin, addressed the assemblage as a whole, reiterating to them their duty to protect the small, still weak American colony they themselves were living in. He then pulled a piece of paper out of his vest, and proceeded to speak in a loud voice: "I have here a letter from Colonel George Chivington, Commander of the famed patriotic Colorado Volunteer Regiment in the late Sioux War in our neighbor then-Territory, now *State...*" Martin paused for effect. "Those of you who have been out here awhile will recall the deeds and sacrifices of that brave unit at Sand Creek in '64. Colonel Chivington, now in retirement in Ohio, sends his greetings and commendations to us, his worthy successors.

'Dear Wyoming Volunteer Regiment,' he writes, 'I am honored to know that you, facing similar circumstances today to those we faced in Colorado in '64, are likewise not standing by, but taking to the field to rid yourselves of the fiends and make safe, for the first time, your habitations and the path into the wilderness west of civilization and your sweet and thriving settled communities. I heartily advise you to take the course we did. Show no remorse, give no quarter to the born killers and brutes. As you go forth, remember my now famous advisement to my men, 'Nits make lice.' Kill them all, regardless how young, aged, or comely they seem! For, all alike are the enemy, hating us, finally, for our way of life, for our freedom, our very civilization! Cut the head off of that snake, skin it, and release it from your thoughts. And you shall find peace! May God speed your progress to this noble end!'"

For the first time in his young life, Chessler thought he knew what a slave must feel like. Only worse—he was, it appeared, deliberately being forced to betray his own highest principles.

No doubt to reinforce his awful feeling of fatal entrapment, "Colonel Martin," still in the saddle, sidled over especially to look him in the eye, clearly emphasizing without a word that he was being assigned deliberately to a hit unit, implying that

Martin didn't much care whether he survived. Edward Chessler's son had never had in his thirty years even a dream as dark and foreboding as this. But he knew he dare not deviate from the vile command.

Following a restless, miserable night sleeping clothed on the bare ground, and with scarce a word exchanged, the tough, somber men of the special unit Chessler was assigned to rose and chewed and swallowed army victuals and swung into their saddles. They were assigned a cannon on a giant wooden-wheeled cart to take to the two pre-scouted encampment sites, under orders to spare no one.

They rattled across the prairie on an old winding dirt track all that day, and encamped for the night on the western slope of a big hill a half mile from the bottoms fronting Rawhide Creek, a tributary of the Platte, where a group of forty or fifty Cheyenne reportedly gathered roots and fished.

A spring rainstorm that turned out more like a deluge for ten minutes came in the night, with furious lightning, thunder booming loudly into the distance, and a brief whistling gale. Chessler, in a tent with two of the others, had noted the storm's rumbling approach for some time. When the blinding and camouflaging monsoon arrived, he slipped out and deftly loosened the bolts on the right-side wheel of the stout cart laden with the monstrous field piece. Then, he slipped back into the tent in the dark, undetected.

When morning arrived, the men, grouchy for lack of sleep and operating on the slippery, rocky ground, started across the intervening long hillside to fulfill their sworn duty. Just as they topped the escarpment and started down into the precipitous ravine, holding back on the heavy cart with ropes lest it get away from them, the loosened wheel gave way, and the whole thing, cannon and cart, toppled, the weight of the stupendous iron piece making it irretrievable.

Then Chessler, feigning skittishness, fired his rifle at a rabbit, in effect warning the Indians below to flee to safety.

How he managed to get word to the Lakota youth encamped a few miles away with their old women root-gatherers the next night to make it into their pitch-dark camp and remove themselves and their whole cache of guns and ammunition has never been disclosed. Nor has proof of his guilt for either. Hobbled, the failed unit dragged back to face Martin.

Though no one could produce any hard evidence, there was a suspicion among the men present, and certainly later by Martin, that young Chessler had somehow caused the series of debacles, probably by bumbling. But with no evidence, no charges were conferred. And so, Martin, left with no choice, and now too busy with his mission, cut loose this strange, quiet man for whom he had formed such a loathing.

3

MARTIN

With the coming of summer in 1876, as Chessler related to Daniel, he resumed his hauling business. The U.S. Army at the fort had never authorized the citizens' militia that Martin, an independent hauler himself, was calling the Wyoming Volunteer Regiment. Inevitably, the majority of the men recruited for it couldn't afford to relinquish their regular paychecks, let alone lose jobs, to participate, regardless of the mysterious all-pervasive threat. In addition, serious command problems quickly arose, and almost at once, it seemed to Chessler, he began to run into a good many of the haulers again on the trails and roadways and at the forts. He himself had gone back to work right away, the Army and Fort Laramie post store lacking an adequate force of teamsters and wagoners.

Later on, hearing that rumors were spreading all over the northern plains that cavalry troops were amassing under Generals Crook and Custer for a great confrontation somewhere up along the ill-marked border between the Montana and Wyoming Territories, Colonel Martin and the sixty men who'd stayed loyal to him headed up that way to contribute needed reinforcements and arms to the coming struggle.

But according to the story Martin himself apparently put out, when they arrived at Fort Fetterman on the way, they were told that General Crook had sent a directive that no civilian paramilitary units were to proceed farther into hostile country for fear such would provoke unnecessary hostilities and perhaps draw the cavalry regiments away from their intended destinations. Even efforts to enlist civilians to the cause were senselessly scotched at Fetterman, according to the fabulist Martin.

The problem with this story, Chessler disclosed to Daniel, was that he ran into Martin riding absolutely alone on the road just north of Fort Laramie on June 17, precisely when the story he circulated had him riding into Fort Fetterman at the head of a column of men. Chessler advised Daniel that he had never before told anybody that, but tucked it away in his head as a reminder.

To hear Martin tell it later (not in Chessler's presence, but he heard about it), the advancing Wyoming Volunteer Regiment, with him in command, could assuredly have turned the tide of battle at Little Bighorn on June 25, 1876, had they only been allowed to advance.

◄►

Old Chessler had what was called a "wild hair" about Martin, his nemesis, who had had more influence over his life from those days onward than anyone else. It went without saying that he was evil and a compulsive liar. The proof was in on that. But Chessler's theory was that Martin lived a sort of double life. He lived an outer life of unimaginable drabness and disappointment, despite having stumbled onto great personal wealth, at least by Wyoming standards. To compensate for the awful drabness of his existence, he had become a sort of artist to himself, who painted a fantasy inner life full of glory, featuring everything he would like to have done in his life.

Thus, he had been a friend and aide to General Grant at Vicksburg. He rode with Bozeman in establishing his celebrated trail and foiled the robbers in the legendary great gold heist on the Cheyenne-to-Deadwood stage road. And now he knew the particulars of Chief Red Cloud's alleged conspiracy to revive the confederacy of the Plains tribes and even yet annihilate white settlement and conquer back their old hunting grounds. Martin knew perhaps because he had ridden over to Pine Ridge and overheard the conversations of the chiefs in the Lakota tongue? Unlikely. Or, perhaps he had his special informants tapped into the singing wire? Whatever the source of the seeds of his fantasies, in real life Martin controlled tight as a drum what went down in Weston County, whether in person or through his personal agents.

But though he indirectly held both himself and Daniel under his thumb, Chessler didn't hate the man. He simply wished he knew how to free the county and the town of Newcastle from Martin's mesmerizing spell. Surely, left to themselves, no one would have believed him or listened to him; but with his money and ownership, most truly did believe and unthinkingly conform to Martin's insistent fables.

Even the often-told story of how he'd come by his great wealth was shot full of holes. According to Martin, after finding gold in the Black Hills, he and Ralph Davis and DeLoss Tubbs got the contract for surveying the route of the Burlington Railroad that was building in from Nebraska. (Other sources said that Frank Mondell was actually one of the three, something Martin unaccountably ignored, and Mondell avoided talking about it, as per agreement.) They stumbled upon this black stuff in the ground on one hill—"black gold" they called it—that turned out to be coal. It was just what the railroad would be needing, no doubt, since railroads always did.

But none of those original three had enough money to pay for digging it up. So Martin sold his team and wagon, and then he and the others looked at each other and decided they couldn't lay trust in each other to be partners. And so they staged a sort of poker tournament to see who would be boss and owner, and Martin won it all. Davis and Tubbs, along with the reportedly somewhat subdued Mondell, went to work for him. Davis's folks came from Wales, and so they named the tough little coal miners' town Cambria. And Tubbs had his own coal camp, Field City, that everybody called Tubb Town.

Martin built Cambria overnight to house the drifters coming in to man the coal mines (disappointed Black Hills gold seekers, most of them). And when the railroad came in a couple of miles west of there in '89, Martin determined to have the whole kit and caboodle moved west and christened it "New Castle" to flaunt his own supposed English ancestry. Martin's coal mines produced all that was needed on the spot by the new railroad line, just about as fast as it could be chiseled loose.

And that's how Martin, for all his sadness and darkness, gloom and rage, ended up "richer than Croesus" and able to buy up every dad-blamed thing and blade of grass in Weston County.

Not that wealth alone made him any kind of a leader. Having suffered through the first decades of his life as an ineffectual ne'er-do-well of a foul-spirited sort, a painfully shy fellow who seldom spoke above a whisper (unless he got on fire for something and forgot himself) for fear of rebuke, Martin resorted to rule by committee. He hired two capable brothers named Kilpatrick to be his front men with the workforce, which he feared, and surrounded himself with a team of sycophantic yes-men.

Six mornings a week, these ten or twelve old derelicts now occupied the benches along upper Main Street, smoking and hacking, talking and sunning themselves with hats in their laps or askew, or else convened in unlit back corners of one bar or another (avoiding only one dive, the "House of Blazes"), to hold privileged discourse through their beer, hats pulled down, and receive what amounted to instructions. Privately, Chessler dubbed them the "loungers" in remembrance of the so-called "Laramie loafers", old Indian elders who sat around the outer porch area day after day at Fort Laramie in his boyhood, talking and apparently preening, while their fellows on the white-Indian frontier busied themselves.

The temperament of these notables was quite different, though.

Martin's loungers—his dimwitted son Manfred, Gregory, Wanstead, Ed Hanes, a man called "Little Ed", sometimes Frank Mondell if he was around, Bailey, Harrison Tyler, Alfred, Peters, Swan, Cambrough, one or two others occasionally— were, in their sum, the outward means by which Martin could inflict the powerful and purposeful life of his imaginings, garnished lavishly with stupendous claims and demands, proclamations, fiats, and ultimatums, upon the unsuspecting world in his Newcastle orbit. And thus, he gained actual control over his surroundings, mandating by innuendo and suggestion who was in and who was out—and *maintaining* it that way—by finding means to subtly buy the community and render all subject to his terrible godlike will. At least, that was how Chessler, in many ways his opposite number and victim of his mandated disdain, had come to see it.

And now, at the dawn of a new century, one that was surely fated to be more civilized and peaceful, more *grown up*, Martin seemed to have slipped entirely off the edge. Nowadays, he was busy circulating through his associates the notion that old Chief Red Cloud, the Lakota chief who had given the U.S. Cavalry and the earliest High Plains settlers fits once upon a time, had, at the age of 81, called back into being the old Indian confederation. According to Martin, Red Cloud had alerted and was readying them to sweep once more out across the western plains, to wipe out all the settlements and ranches scattered over the land, taking the ranchers' cattle as their food supply. Anyone with a grain of sense knew the Indians were abjectly poor since deprived of the buffalo, and had been broken and scattered onto a half dozen patrolled reservations, but such was Martin's control over the community that the wild rumor of an Indian menace quickly gained traction.

Martin had already sent alerts to the soldiery at Fort Frances E. Russell near Cheyenne, and was at work organizing a restoration of the old Wyoming Volunteer Regiment, reminding all who would listen that they could have saved Custer. And he suggested by letter to the Governor of Wyoming that his old associate and partner Frank Mondell, now the state's congressman—without a day of military service—be appointed head of the State Guard. Did Frank himself perhaps harbor secret military ambitions? Chessler wondered about that. Or, more likely, did Martin merely harbor an overwhelming desire to tag and smear others with his delusions?

As outrageous as his view of reality seemed to be, Martin's method of working toward getting things he wanted done was downright frightfully timid—operating through his cat's paws and remaining behind the curtain. Chessler was sure that the majority of the public in Weston County saw Martin as a kindly and gentle grandfather, who continually gave the town and the county nearly everything it had. They didn't buy his blather necessarily, at least not totally, but thought him well meaning. And, with their bellies full of beef and beer and their conveniences assured, plentiful running water and daily mail for those in town, a library, a newspaper, baseball, a spate of posh saloons, they were content to let Martin reign in his fool's kingdom.

Late in the night on January 13, 1903, old Chessler and Daniel, sitting in the dugout, Daniel trying to read his science lesson by the flickering firelight of the fire grate, heard a hubbub, sort of a whoop-up, over in the direction of the town. Throwing their coats on, they eased together out through the heavy log slat door into the snowy night, to behold on the silvery-sheen rim of the hill toward town a quarter mile away, the inebriated frame of Martin himself, viewed in their mind's eye clad in fringed buffalo garb he seemed to wear for months and an old cavalry hat, rocking forward and back on horseback, first leaning crazily to one side and then the other. At that distance, they could just make it all out. He appeared all the while to be brandishing—of all things—a broadsword overhead, swooshing it around in all directions. Chessler fancied he could hear the swooshes in the air. *Swoosh! Swoosh! Swoosh!* Was he really hearing it? Or, just fancying how it would sound closer up? He wasn't sure. *Swoosh! Swoosh!* Daniel said he thought he might have heard it, too. And, in Martin's wake, also on horseback, followed other loungers, keeping their distance at least far enough to avoid being decapitated.

And then they were gone, riding off into other Newcastle neighborhoods, proclaiming their message loudly: Citizens needed to rally, to revive the old Wyoming Regiment of Volunteers to defend their homes against that cunning "rust-nigger" Red Cloud and his irate hordes. For, it was had on good authority such were gathering outside the Pine Ridge agency right under the eye of John Brennan, a "spineless whelp, agent of sloth and rottenness."

So, would the good citizens at their hearths, and in their four-posters at that hour, take to heart or even *take in* the message shouted by these ludicrous ruffian rascals? Chessler couldn't rightly think that many would. But he couldn't imagine that this new bent would bode well for him or Daniel, uniquely remembering more than clearly the last time the demon in this strange man took up this particular cudgel and somehow emerged a formidable presence. Now, it seemed, Martin had awoken to a full-blown spirits-enhanced, death-dealing pathological miasma.

How such a specter of a man had ever wooed and won a sane wife remained, to Chessler, beyond comprehension. It all left Chessler shaking his head and shivering from the cold and a little twinge of dread. Somehow, he was certain that his impasse with Martin had crossed that awful man's relentless mind that night as well.

And Daniel rightly read his Pa's change of demeanor without a word as he damped down the grate and they readied to head to bed.

The next day, they learned that Martin, tanked-up stiff as a board (contrary as it may be to others' experiences), at some point had toppled from his horse and broken an arm.

4
TWO LAWMEN

The one drinking establishment studiously bypassed and ignored by "Martin's loungers" (the true government of Newcastle in old Chessler's estimation) in their almost daily soirees up along the high end of Main, or Warren, was an elaborate combination saloon, dance hall, and theatre known to all as "House of Blazes," sometimes called "The Castle." This was because these mucky-mucks had had an earlier run-in with that austere house of mirth's proprietor, who was the only man in Weston County its potentates found reason to be even a little bit afraid of.

The House of Blazes's owner was none other than Johnny Owens, the ex-sheriff, who was as complex and enigmatic a man as ever appeared on the High Plains. He had first been an unassuming rancher and then a highly successful roadhouse proprietor down at Chug Springs, near Fort Laramie, after working his way up from Texas by way of Missouri and Quantrill's Raiders in the Civil War.

The latter vivid experience had honed his unmatched skills with a gun and made him little more than a killer in the eyes of some. He was even known to have whipped "Wild Bill" Hickok in a shooting match in Cheyenne. Adding substantially to the list of his fatal flaws according to some was his experience of knowledgeably hiring strings of dance hall girls at more than one of his series of establishments— he'd been the owner of a roadhouse, saloons, various gambling halls, and a dance hall or "hog ranch" or two where no hogs of the porcine variety were raised. And on at least two and probably three occasions, he had taken dance hall girls home with him, become smitten with them, and successively made them his wives for a period of months or years.

John Owens didn't drink, but was known to carouse with outlaws and came to know outlaws and outlaw thinking perhaps better than they did. Yet he maintained a reputation as a kind, decent, and honest man, who always, in a phrase from those days, kept on the right side of the law. And, through the midst of it, he was and remained a flamboyant high-stakes card shark and gambler—the "gambling sheriff." (He had even won his first roadhouse saloon in a card game.)

After the nightmare winter of '86, ruinous for stockmen, Johnny Owens moved north with the frontier to a new town called Lusk and got appointed Deputy Sheriff to uphold the law in that remote new area of settlement well north of the region's center, Cheyenne, first known as "Hell on Wheels".

Before long, though, he lost that deputy's job, due to what may have been a misunderstanding, and moved on farther north. Following the construction of the Burlington Railroad, he gravitated to the wide-open new settlements built on coal: Cambria and its more durable follow-on, Newcastle. And in Newcastle he built his bright new "House of Blazes", this one-of-a-kind host's gambit to provide diversions (or *perversions*, as some would have it) for all, eventually including a theatre. And to further accentuate the complex differentness of the man called John R. Owens, he invariably refused to talk about himself or his past. It was as if he was trying to live something down, but nobody knew what it was. And no one seemed to really know him.

As Weston County broke off from Crook County, in Wyoming's northeast corner, and as the parade of assorted murderers, horse thieves, rustlers, and swindlers continued to pass through, and some of them hunkered down to stay, the good citizens, led by the worried power-brokers, urged John Owens to run for sheriff. The Republican-dominated county committee, consisting mainly of the earliest nucleus of the "loungers," eagerly backed the proven tough guy gunman, opting to ignore that he was an avowed Democrat, who had recently attended his party's state convention to support their cardinal of iniquity, the unchaste Grover Cleveland.

Johnny won election as Weston County sheriff in a walk, and proceeded to clear the town and county of its "bad guys," the roughnecks who'd drifted north in search of an essentially raw and lawless space. He easily cemented a reputation as the rough lawman who cleaned up the county, as well as a grand entrepreneur and terrific host for all. That is, as a self-styled man.

Thus the bigger-than-life Democrat who Martin and the backroom powers had favored out of sheer necessity soon gave them indigestion by becoming a power in his own right. So with the town largely tamed, they withdrew their once-fervent support.

By the end of '92, Martin and company had almost had it with him, and decided that something had to be done to bring down this overly dashing "gambling sheriff." But in the meantime, he had ingratiated himself with the public. So what could they do at that point? Deep in their cups, they cooked up a very bizarre scheme.

While Sheriff Johnny Owens was locked in a card game back somewhere within his House of Blazes, on a calm, cold fall Friday night, when the families from all around were in town to shop for groceries and shoes, they would have a giant barrel of slippery oil poured out on the street, as if a barrel toted in a wagon had fallen and burst, right in front of Johnny's door. A big round horse tank would be dragged into place and filled brimful with water a few feet out from the door, with a little incline leading to it, say, for sheep to be able to drink. Then, some fool—maybe a poor soul out of work—would be paid enough to stand there and quickly fire off a round of shots into the sky from a .45 and then duck in somewhere.

And that they arranged and executed, and got it all done without a hitch. In two seconds flat, Sheriff John Owens came flying out through the double doors, toppling tables and pitchers and glasses and patrons on the way. And his hard-heeled boots hit the oil, and he slid straight up the ramp, and loudly—*loudly* splashed into the water of the horse trough. He ended up breaking a tibia, cracking two ribs, and throwing a shoulder out; and when he subsequently came flying up out of the water tank, his pistol registered only a click.

The town was stunned. The street-full of Friday night shoppers were frozen in place. No one moved and time seemed to stand still for ten minutes, while the horse-drawn ambulance came around and bore the silent hero off to the hospital. The brave perpetrators, of course, were nowhere to be seen. But somehow, through his own network of informers, Sheriff Johnny Owens knew almost immediately who they were. Undaunted, he had all the loungers, Martin included, dragged in, swearing and protesting, and clapped into the newly constructed Weston County Jail before morning, every miserable one.

The loungers made a deal with Sheriff Johnny Owens to avoid prosecution. But, it was clear he could not have their backing for re-election.

By the time the election came in 1893, the loungers had talked a younger, but not very conventional possibility, a man of thirty-four, a decent staunch Republican named Billy Miller, into running, even though he, like many others, looked up to and admired Johnny. They used the same argument to persuade him to run that they used with the voters. It was the argument that Newcastle and Weston County were already on their way out of the turbulent and rough old century, filled with run-ins, Indians and bad guys: the pioneer days. And they were headed straight toward a new century of peace and order, out of the century of the gunman and into the century of the decent, law-abiding citizen.

It may have been all right once, they argued, to have a sheriff who shacked up with bar girls instead of attracting and marrying a chaste and respectable wife, one with twenty notches on his gun gained through all manner of shenanigans and circumstances. One who had made his living by selling intoxicating liquors ("poisons" to church folk) and gambling with the riffraff. But now that the chaff had been cleared from the barn, it was time for a family man, a friendly and honest small businessman and stockman, who sold no poison but who had delivered milk from door to door, to represent the town and county and uphold its honor.

The campaign was the fiercest in the county's whole history, as homemade signs full of what were known pernicious lies and insults filled the streets of Newcastle and arguments rang out all over town and out across the open prairies. The election came, and the young door-to-door milkman, the good Christian boy from the Midwest, was elected. And Johnny, no sore loser, was appointed his deputy and went back, most days, to building up his business.

Johnny Owens got along in general with the conscientious and quiet, much younger Billy Miller tolerably well, especially for not being cut from the same cloth and having been thrown together into a heated election. Owens reminded Miller that, with a young family to support, he understood that he had to take advantage of every opportunity. And if the city fathers recruited Miller to run for sheriff, then that was his duty to his family—though it wasn't the safest occupation he might have chosen. Anybody, after all, had a right to run in an election.

The two of them worked together tolerably, too, Billy Miller seeming to appreciate the opportunity to draw on his predecessor's experience, especially with the unfathomable "wild bunch" criminal mind. The two didn't talk much. But, occasionally, one or the other would share a baffling innuendo or piece of rumor that had reached him. One such bit—which Johnny Owens had heard himself—was that Bobby Gammage, the editor of the paper, had had past dealings with Harry Longabaugh, the "Sundance Kid." And allegedly unbeknownst to all, Longabaugh had lodged overhead of Gammage's newspaper office for awhile. Someone said it had to do with something Longabaugh knew from Gammage's wife's past that the editor wouldn't want to get out. The strength of Owens's reputation for honesty was demonstrated by the fact that it was never put around that *he* might have had something to do with the notorious bad man's getting away undetected or with briefly hiding out there.

Billy, as callow as he may have seemed at the start, was a sheriff the whole county could be proud of. Picking up on a tip telegraphed from Montana, the mild-mannered young sheriff arrested a celebrated forger, Philip D. Watkins, who had been staying in a Newcastle hotel under an assumed name, and subsequently learned that the man was wanted by the law in Seattle, Oakland, San Francisco, and Los Angeles. Billy Miller showed that a sheriff didn't have to be the most notorious and fearsome character in the West to keep the town safe and free of scoundrels (with a few exceptions).

As to whether he was a better man than Owens, who was getting on in years and some thought of as a scalawag with friends on both sides of the law—that seemed a matter of opinion. The fact was, both men had won the community's trust and support. Billy was easily re-elected in 1899, and Johnny remained his deputy, and peace prevailed in Newcastle.

The only fly in the ointment that appeared at the ballyhooed dawning of the new twentieth century, hailed as the advent of an era of unheard-of prosperity and civilized living, was the insistent drumbeat by the old reprobates riding out as a rowdy and raucous, drunken vigilante committee, the Wyoming Volunteers. "Reassemble!" their hoarse yells could be heard. "We must bring back to life the Volunteer Regiment now again in our fast-approaching hour of need!" At which point they issued blood-curdling screams and yelps, as if the imagined savages were already upon them!

And on that first dark and cold winter night early in 1903 when the old coots were riding amok in the snow all over town rallying drunken support for a cock-amamie conspiracy about to befall, and a vigilante force to counter it, just as was first conjured and fizzled dramatically forty years before, Chessler shook his head and wondered, "Where on earth is the sheriff?" And, undoubtedly, Johnny Owens, looking out from the doorway of his establishment, thought the same.

But then, the good citizens read in the *Newcastle News Tribune* on a Thursday late in January that Frank Mondell, the congressman hailing from Newcastle, and, when he was home occasionally, one of the loungers himself, was petitioning Washington for five thousand troops to protect the northeast part of the state. And they saw with their own eyes that the Antlers Hotel downtown was being fortified as an actual stockade. So, maybe there *was* something to it!

Could it be that somebody knew something about all this that the general public didn't?

That was the leading question moving forward going into the truly epic year that was 1903. And no one seemed to know the answer.

5

PINE RIDGE LAKOTA

Back in the summer of 1877, a brand-new Black Hills settlement stood on the banks of Rapid Creek. Despite its previous insignificance, it was starting to be known as "Rapid City." If a city is what it was by then, the site was yet so new as to reek of turpentine in the July air.

One of its founders, the successful entrepreneurial prodigy, Irish famine refugee and afterward Iowa farm boy, Major John Brennan who, (though still but 29), was a Civil War veteran, stretched his grasshopper-like long legs under his serviceable old wooden desk in the Aurora House, Rapid City's first hotel and already his second, a 12 X 14 foot log cabin. Brennan was the emerging city's first interim mayor. Also, he had been a member of the place's first, embryonic village council, and was its charter postmaster, president of its first city council, member and president of its first school of mines board, stage line and Union Pacific agent, and the vice-president of the First National Bank of Rapid City all in one individual.

The "hotel" this ambitious young Major Brennan had erected at that time had but one single-occupancy room. And that morning, July 12, in the ebb of the Black Hills gold rush, that room was not yet booked for the night, meaning that Brennan had not yet punched his meal ticket for the day. But a minor bear of a man presently knocked on the door and changed all that. The Major bade him come in, and he cast an impossibly shambling shadow from the doorway behind him, blocking the sun and sky as he staggered forth to enter.

Brennan looked up from his correspondence behind the desk, his bushy eyebrows and broad dust-broom mustache aflutter, it seemed, spontaneously. "Yes?" he inquired crisply of the visitor—by appearances, a bushy vagabond perhaps begging to chop wood for a room, or bringing along some such notion of freeloading.

This uncannily ursine stranger cleared his throat nervously in a sort of irritating high nasal and spoke in what turned out to be tiny and reticent voice: "Uh, M-m-major Brennan," he began, "ah hear tell yore wanton ta hire a hawler, a wagon-man."

"Yes, that's certainly so," Brennan allowed. Jade-eyed, he scanned the dusty and sad-looking ragamuffin up and down, down and up. "And so, what's your story?" he asked, clearly uncomfortable. "And what you been doin' with yourself these last couple o' years, before rattlin' in here, in this far corner o' the world?" It wasn't a capricious question, but rather his way of asking, "Who in blazes are you?"

The disheveled man, a sort of lost waif who'd just burst in out of the nearby barely-formed Wyoming Territory, had himself made a couple of inquiries, and he thought he somewhat knew his man. And here uniquely, presenting himself to a bona fide Civil War officer, he believed his recent background would serve him admirably.

"Do you perhaps remember Colonel Chivington, George Chivington," he asked, "and his Colorado Volunteer Regiment, got up to protect the good people of that then-infant settlement again' the savages?" He fairly beamed to be recounting this in the presence of a military man—a *western* military man. His military man nodded. "Well, then," he continued, "you may have heard how it was that I myself, sir, started up and led a very sim-u-lar Regiment o' Wyoming Volunteers in the late war 'gainst the fiends hyar'abouts." He extended a wavering hand. "Name's Martin. C-c-c-colonel Martin."

"Why, yes, I do recall a hearin' about that unit, rightly enough," the still circumspect Major, Mr. Brennan answered; but now his voice had become a sort of low growl that would have betrayed his thoughts to anyone who knew him better. (He did recall it well, true enough, having been, apparently unbeknownst to this ruffian nincompoop stranger, a community leader in slightly better-settled Denver before chasing the common dream of gold to the Black Hills, where it was newly-discovered. Also unbeknownst to this raucous-looking Martin, he admired and pleased himself to study the western Indians at length as an avocation, subtly sympathizing with their plight. He had, in fact, heartily applauded the Sioux nation's initially being awarded in perpetuity most of Dakota Territory (minus the Black Hills) and parts of Nebraska for their reservation. But, misread by his petitioner, and somewhat to his surprise, he chose to keep his thoughts to himself for his own reasons.)

"We'll discuss the employment tomorrow, then," he hedged, still managing deftly thereby to collect the overnight rent for the room.

The rank flotsam Martin with that took his leave and vanished for the day, to return from wherever he might find himself to move his bag in at sundown.

And throughout the course of the day, the hosteller kept reflecting back to their conversation, his revulsion growing hourly at this cretin tinhorn calling himself *Colonel* Martin who would gloat and favor himself on the basis of his butchery carried out against innocent people he in fact hated for their way of life, for their freedom.

It happened that a dear, though rather new friend and associate of Brennan, Mr. Nick Kelly—a veritable giant, nearly as tall and broad as a Black Hills pine—was the proprietor of the Red Garter tavern down at the other end of the boardwalk. And Ned was a pleasant, rollicking sort, likewise still a bachelor, who agreed entirely with the Major, it happened, on just about everything that came up.

And so the good Major went to talk to his friend, Kelly, and asked him to help resolve his vexation with this awful rogue ne'er-do-well wastrel vagabond, Martin, whom he recalled he had actually heard tell of during the escapades with the Indians back no more than a year or two. A lot of reflections and true-to-life stories had convinced him that such narrow-eyed bigots were squarely at the root of most or all of the worst disagreements and ruckuses in what was still largely by rights an Indian, as well as being a settler's, West.

So he quickly got Nick into the spirit of the thing, too. He was not surprised to learn that Martin had wandered more or less straight down to Kelly's to get lubed, and Kelly found him to be what he called "mousy" or like a muskrat and rather cold in his slinking behavior. So the two of them talked about it and dressed up Nick Kelly, working most of the afternoon at it, it eventuated, as a sort of humongous giant Indian, decked out in mock war paint and feathers, pinned his hair back, and had him practice pretending to walk like an Indian would stalking game. He preened in a mirror, grimaced, smirked with satisfaction, and the imagined likeness was such that they both laughed till their sides split.

And then, when the moon had come out and crickets were chirping, and the slovenly bigot Martin had come back with his bag to that smallest of the world's hotels and rooms, the gigantic nightmare Indian Kelly came by and lowered himself down from the cabin roof in through the window left open to the breezes and, with a thud, fell upon the loathsome lodger and extracting an awful scream, paralyzed him with an arm and restrained him from reaching down under the bed for his carbine.

And Kelly—the giant "Indian", of the sort he must have most hated of anyone or anything in the world—lifted the disarmed bully, a large man himself, and slung him over his shoulder, securing his baggage in the opposite hand, and carried him screaming, helplessly punching, and yelling all the way down to the deep plunge hole below the mammoth boulder stuck in the middle of Rapid Creek. And, sternly warning that if he ever set foot in Rapid City again he'd be scalped, he flung him headlong downward in and left.

Years later, Major Brennan showed up as one of the longest-serving government Indian superintendents on the Pine Ridge Reservation, the most-substantial single fragment left of the Sioux lands somewhat more magnanimously assigned before the tragic series of wars. And there he was, older and somewhat worldly-wiser, in 1903, the year of the great departure on the northern Great Plains and Pine Ridge, and particularly in Newcastle and Weston County.

And this was the same agent Brennan to whom the tycoon and poo-bah Martin alternatively wrote beseeching letters and railed against by post in the late winter and spring of that fateful year. Brennan must call for more federal troops to patrol and defuse the mounting time bomb that Martin claimed to know all about. He knew, he said, about the native resentment and periodic arousal that, for endless years, *was* Pine Ridge. Brennan must strictly reign in the sly old wolf, Chief Red Cloud and all his blood-hungry, hate-filled minions, and stop the runners to and from the old man from dealings over some planned new outrage to be practiced against the defenseless lonely settlements and ranches of the plains—the citadels of civilization, as Martin characterized them. He must pre-empt the slaughter of innocents that Red Cloud and his allies had, Martin said, sworn to unleash in the autumn, by now but months, even weeks away. The letters came in a stream, sometimes once a week, sometimes two a day.

And, for these entreaties, Martin received *nothing* in reply to his many pleas. And neither did Congressman Mondell, the people's tribune in Washington and Cheyenne, to his.

◄►

Charlie Smith, the Pine Ridge Lakota brave known also as Eagle Feather, was a man of two worlds and two heritages. Other Indians didn't understand allotments or exactly what had fatally befallen them; he did. And because he understood it better, he was able to resent it all the more.

This Charlie Smith was nobody's fool. In his thirties, a fine-looking half-breed, he had been sent East and gone through the school for young Indians in Carlisle, Pa., where he learned a lot, paradoxically, about the ways of the whites, always so mysterious and unfathomable for Indians, at least in the West. It could be because Eastern Indians had dealt with the invader for centuries, while, in the West, close contact had lasted, to that point, for little more than a generation. Charlie Smith/Eagle Feather learned reading and writing and some math while at Carlisle, how the capitalistic market system worked, and about written laws and interests, the meaning of contracts, the meaning of exclusive ownership of land. And he learned notions, especially from other Indians and from observing and dealing with whites, of how these things could be twisted to favor whites and rob and destroy Indians. He learned that most whites thought this proper.

He learned that in this whole land called the United States, if you were white and exclusively owned property and, by the way, happened to be born a male and a good Christian and didn't dissent from the way things were done, you were free and ruled all things directly pertaining to you. If not, you were among the things ruled, and survived at best at the proper white men's pleasure.

A long time back on the reservation, sometime in the late winter of 1903, Eagle Feather/ Charlie Smith knocked determinedly on a big wooden door up a miniature flight of three wooden steps at Pine Ridge. He entered when bidden into the office of the Superintendent in a cinder-block building in the midst of a gravel lawn right at the center of the broad rolling-to-flat zone between the Nebraska Sand Hills and the Dakota Badlands designated the Pine Ridge Oglala Lakota Sioux Reservation. Major John R. Brennan ("Long Neck") greeted him and he took a seat offered in the high-backed leather chair next to the faux regimented high Superintendent's desk.

Brennan, as always, was courteous, but businesslike with this guest. "How's the hunt been goin', Charlie?" he asked as an off-hand way of greeting.

"You know," Charlie Smith/Feather responded, "Chukkers and rabbits, maybe a deer occasionally. Not much game hereabout, Sir, that ain't already been shot at or shot."

"Hmmm...that's so, I reckon. What is it that you're getting at, Charlie? Of course, it's a little bit, shall we say, on the thin side here, mostly 'cause you guys are just too good a hunters."

"Well, you know, they just ain't much to hunt here, whatever the reason."

"So, what's on your mind, my good man? Are you asking for again what I think you might be asking for?"

"Well, we know there's not buffalo in the near side of Wyoming anymore. There is not, because you guys...the developers of the railroad and you wild West pioneers took care of that, by shooting all of them down just like they was ducks. But..."

At this word, Brennan looked up from the doodle he was making with his pencil on a Rapid City newspaper.

"But," Smith/Feather—Feather/Smith went on, "there's still so much more out *there* to hunt, and the land and the air over in the open plains of what you call Wyoming, we call our hunting grounds, from way back prior." He paused and then he added, as to one he thought might listen and see matters reasonably. "And there's the ghost game. Even buffalo are out there, for sure, to see and to hunt in the spirit, as real now for us as they were back before."

A slight smile lighted Brennan's face for a second or two, and then he said, "Okay, maybe, we'll see."

And Charlie Eagle Feather, a reader of souls, left, knowing he had a friend, as much as could be, and not just another cold, by-the-book bureaucrat warden. The subject of a hunt was broached and not dismissed, just as old man Chief Red Cloud had suggested it well could be. The young self-conscious half-brave smiled wanly in at least partial recognition, nodded his head slightly, and departed the dark, close room into the sunlight, satisfied for today.

After he had left, Charlie "Eagle Feather" Smith and the Major both mused, each in the context of his own inherited way of understanding. The Lakota kept musing on how it was that the Lakota, who, along with their brothers, the equally hard-pressed Cheyenne, had dealt Uncle Sam his first stunning defeat ever on a battlefield by native Americans, and yet ended up shunted to this circumscribed patch of barren sand and rock, whereas the losers in that pitched fight had ended up with the air and the sun and the grass and the water under all the spectacular blue of the sky, unbounded in every direction. And why was it the Indians that suffered the penalty of penury and dependence from the loss of the recently vast herds of buffalo that the white men had purposely and wantonly destroyed? One irony was nearly as baffling and unfair as the other, for both were destined to live with both, unequally and in perpetuity.

For the "white man's burden" Charlie/ Feather heard about at Carlisle was really shifted to be a burden borne by so-called "red men". And surely, all of the terrible burden that befell the Oglala Lakota under Brennan's not at-fault superin-tendence would warrant for its bearers at least a respite— that at least—when the time came late in the year. Most certainly, that.

What the Reservation's superintendent, Major Brennan, knew, that Charlie Smith quite likely realized less, was that the federal Dawes Act of 1886, coming only gradually into effect, made the claustrophobic and penurious imprisonment of the majestic and truthfully victorious Sioux steadily, and deliberately, worse and more confining. The effect of that wholesale reconfiguration of Indian ownership of much of the High Plains West was to rip it from the common custody of the tribes and give large parts of it back bit by bit to *individual tribe members* without means to effectively possess or improve the deliberately overly-small tracts.

Thus, the self-sustaining wealth of the native tribes, in the form of a myriad of bison and boundless lands full of grass and game that was ripped away, was worsened further by the effect of that law, and by deliberate design, almost for a certainty. And need for recompense necessitated by a deeply corrupt and larcenous contract supply system for food and materials accompanied the banning of the sun dance and the ghost dance, which further accentuated the Indians' feelings of loss and despair. Many were convinced that nothing less than extinction was their lot, fully-intended and soon.

And no sooner had Eagle Feather/Charlie Smith's shadow departed through the big wooden-frame door than Brennan's lieutenant, Raglan, stepped up and handed him a sheaf of letters, at the top of which Brennan saw the same sort of big brown envelope addressed in large print in black crayon that was the hallmark of correspondence received from that insufferable rascal Martin from Newcastle, a thorn, much complained of, in the earnest Major's side.

Emitting an exasperated sigh, Superintendent Major Brennan fairly ripped open the envelope and beheld its usual stained and barbarous contents close up:

"Sir! Add your wait soom as at once to get us sent serous tropes to gard us in are Wyoming towns most proximet the savidge against the up rise planing by Red Cloud. I kno his mind it dont change even tho hes now had an agency namd for him. We are sore needing an won't sit here idol. Don't side with them. Ive told Mondel too.

Now your warned.

Martin"

6
DOGIES OF NEWCASTLE

According to the United States Census of 1900, Newcastle, eleven years into its existence, was a significant town of around a thousand inhabitants, the seat of a new County (Weston) with three thousand residents, in a mostly-empty ten-year-old far-flung frontier state with ninety-two thousand residents in all. Newcastle (or "New Castle," as it was originally printed) was the successor alongside the new Burlington rail line of Cambria, a slightly earlier camp town built on coal mining to fuel the incoming iron horse. The original inhabitants—Sioux, Cheyenne, Crow—were gone from the vicinity less than a generation. The land around was now over-grazed by cattle and far more than a goodly handful of sheep, tended by a trickle of mostly recent-arrivals on ranches. Forts in the region had defended the early trails, roads, and camps from the red-hot angry eventual dispossessed—particularly while the assumed inexhaustible herds of bison, the Indians' cattle, were being wiped out, ostensibly for sport. These forts now were flickering out and left to crumble before the rarely ceasing winds and the onslaughts of blizzards.

But the many pitched battles of that recent era were not forgotten a wit by those surviving who had dug in and raised the standard of civilization as they knew it, mostly settled now in miniature towns and here and there on the land.

And Daniel, Old Chessler's strapping good boy, living at the edge of Newcastle, started to notice, in bone-cold February of the momentous year 1903, a peculiar dotage devoted to the lower right leg on the part of his private and self-possessed Pa. It didn't seem to hobble him, whatever the cause was, and he didn't talk about it. But Daniel noticed it was definitely *something*. Daniel noticed that he spent time alone with it, mostly at night, and the boy presently saw that he had gotten a tin of salve that he was dabbing on.

But by day, he was still himself—and whenever Daniel didn't have to be in school, he and his Pa hitched up the team and went with the dog Red over to the cabin and spring. They headed on the road east on those days, all around the south side of town, to where the old stage road hugged the rim of the minor canyon, above the course of the creek. There, they manned the flowing-spring pump for the occasional traveler. Otherwise unnoticed, as far as they ever knew, they often stopped to say hello, maybe buy eggs or pick up oven-fresh and still hot loaves from a couple on a ranch on the way, John and Luella Church, who were among their few steadfast friends. And, of late, they had made the nodding acquaintance of a drifter who had come there and been taken on as a wrangler and hand by the generous couple, a tight-lipped, seemingly harmless bloke named Clifton.

Part of the bond between the Churches and Chessler was that they, too, were not unfriendly to Indians and sheltered one or more occasionally coming through. Chessler and Daniel cherished the association.

And then, all of a sudden, the hospitable and kindly Churches were gone.

Old Chessler mused on the day, before they'd heard the sad news, that he'd just stopped at the Churches' pleasant doorstep, alone while Daniel was in school, and found them not at home. The barking dog was gone with them, and Chessler surmised that they'd probably gone along to town to buy groceries and perhaps sit, all three of them, for an hour at Johnny Owens's silent film palace. Old Chessler chuckled as he drove the horses over how they'd argue endlessly the merits of the two sheriffs, Owens and Miller, the old dead-eye, colorful and potent one, versus the young, wholesome family man, arguably a better example starting out a new, civilized century of prosperity.

He couldn't help but chuckle about how John and Luella forever argued, even if it was thumbs up versus thumbs down, just to be arguing and stimulating one another, though it was obvious they loved each other dearly. And then how they—too readily, he thought—took in the odd, down-on-his-luck stranger Clifton almost as their son, even though they were all close to the same age. Chessler missed their company and cheeriness that day, as he drove along toward the canyon and the cabin and the well where he had eked out a bare subsistence and maintained his independence into near old age.

And then, he overheard in town one day soon after that the Churches had gone missing and that the drifter Clifton was suspected in their disappearance. Clifton's alleged involvement somehow didn't surprise Chessler much, even though he hadn't thought of such a thing as a possible explanation himself.

But Chessler wasn't necessarily buying it, either. It's true that "Slim" Clifton—or "Diamond Slim" or "Diamond L Slim", as Chessler discovered—was odd and an enigma. It was possible, though not probable, that he had harbored some ill will toward the kindhearted Churches. But Chessler also recalled hearing about how John Church, with Luella right by his side, had stood outside Johnny Owens's House of Blazes near the top of Main Street and roundly denounced the tycoon Martin's re-organizing of the so-called Wyoming Volunteer Regiment, in effect a mob got up to go after any Indians who would dare to come into eastern Wyoming. Church had argued passionately, unadvisedly shouting for all to hear, that there was no threat, that the Indians, now penned up like so many sheep at Pine Ridge and other places, were themselves the victims. And Chessler, who had learned his lesson and kept quiet, after not-so-subtle threats, knew how vindictive and crazy mean Martin, the tycoon-tyrant of the town, could be.

But would Martin actually have a dissenter killed over it? Well, wouldn't he? That was the likely result with a rabid bigot who owned the town. And he was a rabid bigot! And he did own the town! Then, he'd lay it onto a scapegoat.

And Clifton, who owed the Churches some money, would've been an easy target for that designation. True, it was said—*they* said—that Slim had owned up to it. But could that be right? Because why in blazes would he have done it? Too many questions!

Nevertheless it was Clifton who was thrown into jail with a trial date set.

Meanwhile, old Chessler had his own problems—primarily, the vexing, more-than-likely malignant, quarter-size wound on his lower right leg, the origin of which he couldn't recall or easily imagine, either.

It may have started from a scratch by one of the cats that hung around out in the tool shed, who clamored crazily around him when he brought the milk from the cow back to the house and deliberately spilled the top of it off in their pan. But he'd also seen mean-looking spiders scurrying in the shadows in that same old lean-to, hairy and black and the size of a silver dollar. Now, if one of those rascals had latched onto his leg while he was out and about…Snake-bit, he didn't suppose. No, it was more than likely that over-zealous little orange cat, its way of being friendly, lusting for milk and attention.

Downed by a milk-shed cat! It seemed that well could be!

Nicks, bullet grazes, dings, scabs, and scratches galore he'd had, but Old Chessler had never had a sore that wouldn't heal by itself. This one, in fact, seemed to just get worse. All he could manage to do was try to keep it clean. Sort of instinctively, he put alcohol on it and rubbed Dr. Crowe's Salve in and wrapped it in gauze bandages as best he could. But three inches above his right ankle on the outside of his leg, it stayed red and sore around its raw, ragged edge, and dead-feeling and welling with pus down in the middle of it, in its crater, as he visualized things he couldn't view straight on. And when he poked at the raw red rim, it stung as if he'd grabbed hold of a single nerve cord with tweezers or sliced the same with a razor, making him wince and gasp audibly—a gasp and a grimace young Daniel had picked up on by the light of the fireplace. Of course, it began to worry the both of them. But Daniel didn't ask about it just yet.

And it didn't hobble Chessler or slow him down, except a time or two when his unprofessionally applied bandages trailed down his pant leg and flowed out behind him, once with Daniel there to see it and exchange a silent, sympathetic frown with him as he perched on a rock to readjust matters.

Finally, the second time an embarrassment like that happened, Daniel spoke right up: "Pa, why don't you go to a doctor with that?"

And old Chessler sighed deeply. "I did, son. If I'd a stayed, I'd still be sitting in the waiting room there at the hospital. That's how we know they'd been warned of us, same as with the Churches."

Whether Daniel's sigh and shaking his head was a mimic of old Chessler doing just the same, or merely the only response available to him, could have been grist for one of the Churches' pointless friendly arguments. Senseless and perverse as it surely was.

Chessler thought about the Churches and started to smile as he drove out alone another day. Then, he remembered that the friendly and mild, steadfast Churches were probably dead, and their crazy hired man locked up in jail for it. And, he might soon join them, one way or another, if his dang sore didn't heal. Brought down by a milk-shed cat! There was assuredly no other response on earth to *that* than to shake his head, the Churches dead and gone or not.

And Chessler thought back on what fine and courageous friends the Churches always were to him—almost the only he had in recent years in Weston County. Not so very long ago, he had come into that newly opened country from the chalk and bone country down to the south along the Platte and around Fort Laramie. Not too long after arriving, after dabbling over in the spotty Black Hills gold ground, as most thereabouts had, he was over at Edgemont across in Dakota on a wagon trip and brought back the baby from there, Daniel, who no one else he could find would have anything to do with.

He recalled that the child was clearly not doing well on such milk as he could manage to get—even the milk from Billy Miller's dairy cows, at the time. And so, he'd asked about in despair, ranch house to ranch house. Finally he was directed, and none too soon, to the Churches, someone knowing that Luella had nursed a newborn son that recently died.

The Churches then had been unpopular for harboring the Indian wanderers who came through, and giving them ranch work. But Mrs. Church, as distraught as she was for losing her own child, agreed to try to suckle Daniel. It was something the boy would never be told. But, together with the understanding of and seemingly instinctive trust by Indians, it provided the bond that bound those four as perpetual friends.

And, was that slightly twisted stranger Slim Clifton powerful enough to break such a bond? This was a question Chessler pondered, while somehow thinking that Luella might have known what to do to heal up his leg, had he but ever thought to ask. And that only they, as far as he could know, knew his secret. And now, as far as was known to him, only his boy Daniel, among the living in Weston County, knew.

He wanted to go by the jail and ask Diamond Slim himself if he had really done it, but knew it would mark him. He lacked the foolhardy courage that only the Churches among all he knew would have had. But he felt he owed it to them—yet, what good would it do anyone if he were hunted down afterwards? And he knew he would be, if his pure but nevertheless strong hunch that Slim had been set up, were right.

He couldn't help remembering in this connection back to the time Martin had sent his worthless drunken son, known as Manfred, out to take care of the "Indian-coddling" Churches. This was the same husky dolt who not long before had, for no reason whatsoever that anyone had ever been able to divine, charged his horse at full gallop up the steps of the big square-block Weston County Court House, continued on at full-tilt inside the building, and would have inevitably crashed up against the north interior wall if one of the clerks had not conveniently jumped over to throw open the little-used north door to let the bolting steed exit. But for Manfred, unfortunately, this second door was not nearly high enough to permit the rider to pass safely through as well. The result being that he cracked the plaster above the door with his forehead, ripping his hat, and he himself suffered a cracked skull—and hadn't been the same for a single day since. He now worked zombie-like to carry out his father's every wish because he lived in terror of him.

Manfred's twin, Thomas, a good and thoroughly decent man of hardy good cheer, an honest lawyer and benefactor to the community, had been shot in the head a year before and his body thrown into the weeds behind the Court House. No solid evidence was ever found, but rumor had it that Martin had been behind it because

Thomas had known too much of Martin's business. Now, poor Manfred—if you could pity such a man—seemed to drift in a fog, with little knowledge of the past that wasn't horrific, and without a scruple in his head. He was, in effect, a monster trying to escape the wrath of a far more cunning, soft-voiced monster who scrawled and handed him crayoned instructions he strained to read on bar tabs or in the margins of the weekly *News-Journal*. Thus, he was both actually pitiful and much to be feared, likely as not to do anything at any time. At times, however, he seemed pleasant and quite lucid, so one just never knew.

On the occasion of this son of Martin's punitive mission to visit the Churches, this same poor horse somehow ended up with his steel-hard hooves breaking the wood plank casing above that couple's otherwise open well. Manfred ended up at the bottom of the well and had to be fished out at the end of a rope thrown down to him by none other than the Churches themselves, both equally powerful, who responded to his cries and pleas for help.

The horse, miraculously, did not break a leg in the ordeal. Chessler surmised that his extraordinary good fortune was due to the unusually high limestone content underlying the particular pasture where the horse generally ran free. Chessler, a good judge of mules and horseflesh, thereafter vowed to buy that unfortunate beast for himself should it ever come up for sale.

With a wound that stung, day and night, like a jagged piece of rusty iron impaling him, or, at times more like a cigar snuffed out on his bare leg, Chessler needed to try to direct his thoughts elsewhere. Weighed down with the ugly fate of his friends, too, he couldn't avoid concluding that John and Luella would probably still be alive were Johnny Owens still the sheriff to deter Martin. He wasn't the only citizen of Weston County who at times still pondered why it was that a superior lawman and a good man had been replaced by popular vote. Chessler reminded himself that it was Martin saw to the counting of votes, and because Johnny had begun to replace Martin and his bunch as the authority in the county, and neither Martin's son nor any of his other lackeys was man enough to change that violently.

But, that much being said, how was it that the elevation of the virtuous novice, in the still half-wild town and vicinity had been made, by all appearances, to appear above board and to succeed? Luella Church, Chessler reflected, had had a notion about that herself. An Owens partisan, she had held that it was the vote of the *woman*—the reputedly tamer gender—that had made the difference. Wyoming being about the only place, of course, where it could have mattered, since the vote for women had been the established law first and uniquely in Wyoming since the earliest territory days, over thirty years ago now, and was by now virtually taken for granted. (And, of course, Luella and John had argued endlessly the virtues of *that* fact to pass the time, too).

But then again, Chessler fondly pondered, the Churches were among the most enthusiastic patrons of Johnny Owens's picture show in his later annex to the House of Blazes. Johnny, he knew for certain, knew and appreciated them, too, and would not have let them ever become a lethal target of Martin's blind bigoted fury—or himself either, for that matter, he supposed.

Sheriff Billy Miller would never have wanted such a thing to happen either, but may have concluded that he had to just permit some things he didn't like to go on.

Still, none of Chessler's musings got him one whit closer to unraveling the mystery of Diamond Slim. Where did the man even come from? And if he did do it, was it on his own impetus, or had some power coerced him?

7

THE EARS AND EYES OF JOHNNY OWENS

What Johnny Owens, the multi-interested ex-sheriff who cleaned up New-castle before the Martin crowd scuttled him in '98, actually thought of Martin was not public knowledge. But like Chessler, he had come to the conclusion that most of the illicit activity in Newcastle was the work of the secretive looming tyrant. Martin generally did none of his own dirty work, but stayed hidden behind the persona of a sort of inarticulate grandfatherly philanthropist, quiet and bumbling, acting through cats' paws and fawning lackeys competing for favor and advancement. The likelihood that Johnny regarded Martin as the worst and maybe the slyest skunk-gorged sidewinder of the hundreds he had dealt with in his rocky career and life he chose to keep private.

Johnny continued to focus a proprietary eye on the goings-on around town. He saw plenty for himself in his roles as deputy and saloonkeeper, but the other saloon men kept him apprised of everything afoot, including Martin's drunken mumblings and grumblings. Thus he knew what was going on in Newcastle perhaps more than any other one person.

He also heard rumors from the Sheriff Miller, the most significant of which lately was that apparently Mr. Gammage, the newspaper editor, had wanted to talk to "Diamond Slim" Clifton in the jail to see if there was anything to the speculation that the debt of money he was said to have owed the Churches could have been a motive for their murder. And if not, had someone put him up to such a thing? When Gammage shared with one of the clerks in Martin's store that he had a notion to interview Diamond Slim, the rumor went, the clerk answered with the frank opinion that people in Newcastle didn't want to hear about crazy conspiracies like that, and someone might just be upset enough to set fire to his news office if he stirred up unfounded talk of such nature.

John Owens just shook his head on hearing that one. There might be a kernel of truth in it somewhere, and an illegal threat was also possible. But there was simply no way of knowing for sure. And if it were true, divulging and attempting to prosecute it could destroy the whole town. As was often said, he reminded himself again, sometimes even a rotten house is better than no house at all. But, could it, for all of that, be true? Owens wasn't sure.

Another rumor the former sheriff had heard was that Martin had induced someone in the Wyoming Legislature to request a name change from Weston County to Martin County. This one very well could be true. But, according to his informant, the legislature was not moved to make such a change, but voted merely to memorialize their tycoon patron on the advice of Congressman and one-time Governor Mondell, Newcastle's other prominent son.

Old Chessler recalled how it was that he first laid eyes on Owens back in or around 1880, when that already-famous gambler and honest gunman was running a gambling hall and sin parlor at a station on the stagecoach road just east of Fort Laramie known as Three Mile. For some reason that nobody seemed to be able to fathom, a set of would-be highwaymen confided in this rough-cut owner of the establishment on that occasion that they intended to waylay and rob the northbound stage coming up from Cheyenne carrying payroll for the Black Hills at Eagle's Nest, a location a good distance farther north. As it happened, Chessler, for the first of a very few times in his life, had signed on to drive that stage for part of the way to its destination, when the regular driver inexplicably reported in sick; which is why he happened to be there at Three Mile. The terminus of the run was Deadwood, a few score miles past where Newcastle would stand not much later.

As the time of the stopped stage's departure neared, after the desperados had gone out the door and away from his premises, a much-younger Chessler watched as Johnny literally pulled off his apron and slipped it on the man who had been riding shotgun, whom he didn't know in the least, strapped on his pair of six-shooters, grabbed his rifle, and traded places temporarily with the startled guard.

He rode next to Chessler up the line, and they exchanged pleasantries and a carefree laugh or two. Then, when the three desperados appeared, Chessler quoted him in later years as saying in a familiar, almost friendly tone of voice, the rather standard theatrical "Not today, boys." Chessler watched in stunned silence as he cut two of them off at the kneecaps with three nearly-silent rapid-fire shots, and saved the stage and Chessler's and two startled passengers'—both sleeping uniformed soldiers—lives. The third rider whirled and sped away to the north, quickly galloping out of gun range.

What Johnny didn't know at the time, though, was that the plot also involved another part of the same gang who were later that day, perhaps to benefit from causing confusion, to rob a gold shipment stage coming down the road south from Deadwood. The escaping rider, though, did know and sped up the line and warned his fellows that Johnny Owens, well-armed, along with two soldiers on the boot, were on their way.

Unknown until days later to Chessler, who had ended his own contract role as driver at Lance Creek, the gold stage robbers, who had already hijacked the southbound stage, apparently then looked for a place alongside the road to ditch their treasure, in the form of five-hundred gold bricks, in order to recover it later. Their thinking was that the famous gunman, taking his role as a citizen and protector of a friend's stagecoach seriously, would have no reason to interfere with them without the slightest evidence of a theft.

But when Johnny's northbound stage rode beside that coach, the driver of that other rig touched his hat conspicuously twice, a signal Johnny recognized as meaning gunplay had accompanied a robbery. Johnny was ready, and indicated he was taking charge. The shootout that resulted left both of the culprits critically, though not mortally, wounded. Johnny Owens, a man without a badge, took the two prisoner on the driver's testimony. But the poor, brave driver was also shot in the dust-up and, after lingering and stating that the gold bricks had been dumped in a deep ravine he wasn't able identify, died.

Chessler, for his part, was amazed for years afterward that his deadly and mostly taciturn companion on the earlier part of that trip had contented himself with merely filing a public report of the incident and returning to the menial work of running his business, apparently never bothering to hunt for the gold. Only later did he realize that to have done so would have tarnished this most remarkable man's honest, though delicate, reputation. Still, Chessler had always suspected that John Owens had watched and looked after the site of the drop and might even have moved to the now community of Newcastle because of it.

Old Chessler had merely glimpsed Mr. Owens's comings and goings occasionally over the years, and the two had only exchanged a word or two in passing before they both arrived in the same town within a year of each other. Most recently, Chessler had read in the *News-Journal* that local sportsman John Owens had taken his prized filly, Nellie Stotts, down to Alliance and beaten the local champion horse there, Ten Pin.

As for foiling the double robbery and the harrowing day traveling together, Johnny had never again mentioned it to Chessler, and Chessler had never brought it up.

PART II ➤ SPRING

8
GAIETY & STEALTH

The good folks of Weston County did not do proud the most consequential and indispensable officers of the chief town and surrounding land of treasure and thinner air, namely their sheriffs. In fact, they housed them, utility-like, in a sort of annex to the jail.

But Anna Miller, as much as she shed tears at the thought of feeding and bedding her precious and ample family in such grim surroundings as the local clink, was nevertheless the envy of many a struggling worthy lady in the fast-maturing and lively little city of Newcastle. Was there danger in keeping her darling brood of seven, counting herself and the mister, under the same roof, though separated by a wall, with murderers and horse thieves and burglars armed with pistols and two-barrels?

Whether that was prudent or not (and events would soon prove), the prisoners did have to be moved in and out, at least, within mere feet of her children. And, should there come assaults on the holding pen, from within or without, well, then, *who could really say?*

But she did her utmost nonetheless to make it a fitting home. And, within the parameters of what she had, she succeeded admirably. Her three youngest, Sidney, Raymond, and Ruth, 7, 6, and 3, were only told that those were "cowboys," lest they cry and be afraid.

Were there desperados who conducted themselves with more civility on the premises in custody, knowing there was a lady with five little ones practically in their midst? Most assuredly, some would or did. But it was also up to her to provide the meals for them, as well, meaning that for others, reasonably good conduct would have been the only option.

Late one weekday afternoon in April, with old snow still lingering, her Billy, to her at times just a bigger version of her Raymond and Sidney, came in unusually cheerily, breezily almost, stomping snow briskly off his boots. She divined that something was surely in the offing. Squeezing her almost too tight, in a gesture that was, for him, kind of exuberant, he grabbed a big handful of peanuts from the stand under the stair landing and stuffed his face full.

"*Eeeee!* What's happening?" she exclaimed. "What's going on? What on earth?"

He had to pause and chew for almost a minute before answering.

"Mresunts nguming," he answered, or something like that.

"What? What did you say?"

He chewed as fast as he could and swallowed in a gulp. "President's coming," he repeated cheerfully.

"What?" She still didn't exactly get it.

"President Roosevelt is coming here to Newcastle!" he announced again. "He'll be here in less than a month now!"

She had never seen her man beam more proudly. It was big news, she had to acknowledge, but only he among adults would likely view it as a child. And she understood! Understated as her Billy was, he perked up predictably to his own set of cues, pertaining solely to him.

Three-year-old Ruthie came scooting in from the more private areas of the apartment and clung to her father's legs, nearly pushing him off-balance. He picked her up and, kissing her neck and touching softly her chin, he swung her around and pulled her to him for a second and
set her down, to scurry off again following her mother's skirt toward the kitchen.

And the sheriff, a callow young man who had earned the respect of the would-be lawless, plumped seat-first deep down into a welcoming overstuffed chair. As the welcoming aroma of gravy and beefsteak wafted to his appreciative nostrils, his wife flitted past him to beckon the older children come in from their game of tag just outside the door.

Tonight, the little family of Weston County's sheriff seemed to draw together a little more closely than usual, seeking respite from a somber shadow they unexpectedly felt themselves under, in the veritable presence of a likely murderer agonizing his fate.

Diamond Slim was in a cell sealed off by impenetrable, fortified walls, but as all of them except possibly little Ruthie were aware, just a matter of feet away from their own bright and comfortable asylum.

◄►

Uptown that night, in the barroom lounge of the Antlers Hotel, the informal shadow council of the town, the loungers, chaired by the wily eccentric tycoon

Martin, were assembled in their chairs after their dinner cups and plates had been pushed back, to discuss and, as it turned out, strategize local human fate.

Present there in addition to Martin himself were Manfred, at Martin's right hand, an old horse trader from down on Beaver Creek in a trademark black top hat everyone called Jake (though his given name, known to a few, was Taylor Filmore), Ed Moulder, Bailey, the peppery Little Ed, and a callow and fawning man they sometimes put up with named Patrick (or "Old Rick"), said to have been Martin's daughter-in-law Iris's first husband.

Bailey, the jeweler, assumed his usual spokesman's role for Martin, who normally couldn't project his voice beyond a barely intelligible mumble these days. (Many suspected he had throat cancer.) The spokesman's flat tone did not come off as the friendliest tonight: "Anyone who cannot or will not keep what we say here to himself had best leave. Or we will find us a way to leave him." Bailey paused, and then intoned: "If we are at all serious again about mounting up our Wyoming Volunteer Regiment and protecting our towns an' ter...state, then, we've got to deal with open dissidents coddlin'...shall we say, Injun lovers?"

Everyone at the table, save Bailey and Martin, said "um-hmmm" and nodded.

"An' that's what we done." He looked around at them and Martin had scooch-ed down in his chair, almost under the table, and, continuing to loll, drawing on his long-stem pipe, which he clutched in his two hands, sort of mouse-like.

"...In such a way," Bailey continued to drawl on, "as to not alarum the popu-lace...that is, to make it look, in each an' evry case, like someun else done it. But we gits the benefits, see, of not havin' to deal wif the Indin-coddlin' scum-buckets."

"And so then, what about that old Chessler feller out thar on the edge wif that boy?" Little Ed wanted to know. "How's he git off, when we know, all of us, how he's a-feelin' sorry fer the devils that practicly razed him? If I'm understandin' it at all aright."

Martin, it was noticed by more than one, had developed a sort of grimace, a look of distaste, on his unique crinkled face, viewed now just above the level of the table top, raising just a fleeting suspicion he might have suffered a stroke.

"Well..." Bailey, not really having an answer at that time, let the mention of Chessler trail off for the time being.

"But, what if that Cliff, er Slim, decides ta talk at the trial?" Ed Moulder, the liveryman, brought up.

His decidedly louder voice made everyone check all around, to make sure they weren't overheard.

Martin mumbled something to Bailey, taking almost a full minute, during which the others leaned in, trying in vain to hear what he said.

"Well, ya know what?" Bailey then started in again, a little more loudly himself, "we was sposed ta spring Clifton. Leastwise, that's what we tol' 'im we would do."

"Yeah," they all exhaled around the table.

"Well, we'll spring 'im alright," Moulder affirmed. "Into whichever way he's headed. But not so's he's gonna talk and tell. Either at a trial. Or thereafter, either."

A long silence ensued, as big Ed Moulder cast a searching eye around the table, from one to the next to the next, until all had tumbled to what he meant. And some audibly sighed, all of them realizing that there was no other way it could be done.

"So, how we gonna git 'im out past the sheriff?" Little Ed wanted to know.

Bailey and Martin conferred again. Bailey smiled, almost cheery, upon learning from authority how it could be done. "We wait," he said, "until that bizness and ceremony with TR, the president, is in high gear. That's when we jist waltz him out, while our good Sheriff Miller is all taken up wif the rigamarol."

"What then?" Little Ed asked, sounding almost dumb to not quite get it even yet.

"Well..." Bailey answered, this time thinking on his own, "we'll jist see. Jist wait and see." At the end, there was just a hint that his patience was about at an end.

He looked around at every one, one by one, again. And then he gave a little laugh. And then he spoke again. "We cain't leave the fate of sich a cold-hearted murderer up to a soft-headed jury, with not all of it even of the masculine pisuasion, now can we? *Hmmmm?* Nor, up to the wiles of a fancy-word lawyer, *right?* They're jist about bound to let 'im off if we do, ain't they?" More resolutely now, he continued, "We've got to make damn sure they's *justice* dispensed, an' no mis-take, eh? *Eh?*"

Now he was smiling again, and Martin, slid right down next to him, was grinning ear-to-ear, appearing oddly to crack up from... something. And his right eyebrow kept twitching rapidly. Bailey winked, and all laughed, but uneasily, upstanding community businessmen that most of them were.

◄►

Chessler had suffered from the deep, mysterious, possibly cat-caused wound which had progressively worsened for three months now. Though he kept it as clean as he could with bracing baths of rock salt in mineral-laden water and applied dabs of the pungent salve he'd bought at the mercantile, it had developed a worrisome low-grade infection that seemed to be graying a bit in color and eroding back the tissue surrounding the round, intensely-sore deep crater of it.

And lately, he thought he detected a touch or course of fever in the night running into early morning. If he'd had a few more coins safely tucked in an account, he might have taken a stage or perhaps a train to the Ivinson Hospital in Laramie, or even to Denver, to have it properly attended.

But then, what would happen to his livestock, not to mention his son Daniel, while he was gone—or, if he was gone permanently? That, he hadn't figured out. And no one was friend enough to share his burden with—all were scared onto the cautious side. Only the Churches had always remained his brave friends, the rest being differently disposed, as they were, for good reason he reckoned.

But what would become of him, he didn't know. He just kept on binding the problem leg up in bandages and salving it, more than anything to hide from Daniel the bare-faced ugliness of it, reflecting all too well the condition of the life he was forced to endure.

But Daniel was as smart as they come. "Pa, what makes people do things that are so gall-dang mean?" he questioned out of the blue one night.

"So *mean?* Whatever do you mean, son?" Chessler answered.

"I mean, like with Slim, Diamond L. Slim, they say was his full name, and what he did to John and Luella?"

"Well, did he? What makes you so sure it was him that did such deviltry? You tell me."

"You're right, Pa, and I was thinkin' he didn't seem like he would. But, whoever would?"

"Well, son, I figger it's like, everybody's got so much boring time on their hands—hereabouts, at least—where nothing much is happening, for or against 'em, runnin' on for days and days sometimes. And, if they're not too careful, or don't care particularly, their natures fill in the spaces, and plum overthrow 'em.

"People get ideas in those intoler'ble gaps in time that won't stand up well to logic nor reason, sich as that some folks is jist better than others for some gall-dang fool reason. Like, there's people who want to think that's true, and even sometimes stake their whole lives on it being true, to make sure the others who they decided to be against don't get an advantage over them in some way and maybe prove they're not all that much as they pretend themselves.

"And then, once they've made a mistake of acting out that there fatal life decision—that is, their hatred for someone, it amounts to in some a them—they think they have to act like that, sometimes again and again, in defense or to proclaim the craziness in their head that led them to that bit of nastiness, as being right and true. Or else, to try and cover up or deny that they said it. Or did it." He stopped to reflect.

"So, if there's one thing I know to pass on to you, it's this: allas own up to what you did, be it good or bad. And if you see it as bad later, turn from it. You don't have to ever defend it."

"Pa," Daniel asked, "do you think he did it?"

"Yes, and no, Dan. Yes and no."

Daniel thought for a long moment, and then nodded in agreement.

And Chessler determined he would have to go and ask Diamond Slim that very question shortly himself.

Meanwhile Daniel, Chessler's fawning, sensitive boy, endured with difficulty the late-winter days of 1903, filled with worry and tumultuous events, by projecting daydreams onto developments out in the world at large he read of each passing week in the pages of the *News-Journal,* printed right up near the top of Main Street.

He read of the deal to tap an oilfield a little west of town with one of the first oil derricks in the state, and knew it meant more wealth for Martin, the only local man with enough money to invest substantially. He read in those pages of the aviation experiments first of the Brazilian Santos Dumont in Paris, then of Edison, and now of someone named Wright on the east coast. And he imagined how such an air ship could more easily find updrafts to hop from one butte to the next in the western landscape, where the air would be less dense. And he read there in those pages of a certain doctor down in Lusk who had imported the first horseless carriage into that part of their state.

Indeed, with the forthcoming wonders of the twentieth century ahead, the Wyoming Volunteer Regiment's talk of Indian-hating seemed to him delusional twaddle, based on a vision firmly stuck in a more sordid, if storied, past.

On two successive nights following, Martin, drunk as a proverbial lord (in actual fact no shrinking violet, though he pretended so and some privately adjudged him a coward without his cups), held forth standing up on the front of a flatbed wagon pulled up and parked near the top of Main Street across from the court house. He proclaimed in that rasping drunk voice of his, distant and hollow, through the biggest bullhorn anyone had ever heard or seen: "Do not deny the reality of Red Cloud, but rise up and defend your towns and countryside from the hordes mounting up again at the east! They're ready to ride down on us like the terrible Turks of old!

"They propose to have their way with our cattle and our women! Arise and join the Regiment of Volunteers, my dear, good friends, anew! Let all of the true men in the sound of my voice arise now and join! Arise and join! Arise and join!" His voice reverberated and silence prevailed for a moment, then: "Come, arise and join us now, or on the Court House lawn and steps tomorrow at noon!" Pause. "Let each and all of you who cherish and honor your wives and mothers and children and fellow man come and join us so we can scour and scourge clean off the face of the land and earth and make straight the way, and let us maintain watch on our borders, lest the fiends again slip in out of Dakota bringing with them mayhem and death!"

The last word, heard all over town, trailed off into "*Deatttthhhhhhhh...*"

"We have it that they are massing to take up their old hunting and roaming grounds and recover the graves of all their generations, and you with some age on you have seen it and know even as I do it is so! *This is your leader!* Tomorrow, stand with me and deliver—silver on the barrel! We're goin' to crush them when they dare to come across...*again!* Come all and sign! Come all! All! *Allll!*"

The next day, a Saturday, in an early spring misty morning rain, some made their way uptown, crowding in under an awning that was set up, and pledged their service—but without much fervor, and to only a few cheers and little fanfare. Chessler heard about that disappointing partial failure to arouse only much later.

9

THE SENSIBILITIES

Old Chessler had kept abreast as well as he could of developments among the friends of his youth and their spawn, the Lakota people now at Pine Ridge. His eyes and ears for the little he'd been able to glean of their daily experiences and circumstances had been a few lone travelers who had sojourned with the Churches or occasionally stopped for a restful watering and visit in the shade following the stage road to or coming from the graves of the old ones or gathering medicinal plants in an established source.

Perhaps strangely, the Churches had had no other connection to the tribes than just the fact that their parents had come into the country among the very earliest of the whites, and in learning to live from the land, their independent viability had stemmed from the knowledge patiently gained from their aboriginal neighbors. And those venerable neighbors, they learned, not been on the High Plains of the West forever either and had had to learn to survive there themselves from still earlier people.

The Sioux and Cheyenne had in fact shared their knowledge willingly and with deep pride, convincing Chessler that the outcome of contact between the two peoples could have turned out far more mutually beneficial. Plus, anyone who paid any attention knew that the hearty native cattle, the bison, were far better suited to the land, the only drawback being their sometimes difficult high-spiritedness, a trait once shared with their human consorts, who were now equally broken and discarded.

Old Chessler reflected often on a vivid fantasy he'd had when he was young, sleeping in the workmen's quarters at Fort Laramie. In it, he saw enormous, well-tended, even enlarged buffalo herds on the plains, roaming free through careful management and rules made together by Indians and whites, to be hunted and harvested sensibly by all together for subsistence or sale and distribution. In his vision, there were no foreign cattle being widely introduced to overstock the range, beggar the forage, enrich a relative few, or banish the natives. But even then he realized that real and sustained amicability was too radical a notion to be entertained by most of what he called his "*actionista*" brothers, with their cloying lip service to a so-called "Prince of Peace"—well, in life, it was not going to happen.

What he had learned through those occasional wanderers from Pine Ridge—albeit as likely outcasts and malcontents as spirit-brothers—had not yielded the slightest sense of brewing menace or uprising, but only of malaise and despair and lack of means. Earlier, buoyed by idealistic backers from the East and a few somewhat sympathetic ranching neighbors to the south in Nebraska, there might have been fleeting visions of some sort of rejuvenation. But as for where Martin had gotten the notion of a new, threatening surge coming, Chessler could but suspect serious head-sickness and self-serving delusion.

Chessler knew of the government Indian policy controversies that had rocked the Oglala Lakota as well as other Indians dating back a few years, from a handful of letters he had exchanged with reservation friends and knowledgeable others back at the time. He knew of the law pushed through by somebody named Senator Dawes, by which the tribes were to be phased out as well as the reservations, and the Indians to be regarded individually, each deeded a small farming plot and taught to assimilate as farmers and herdsmen—not far from the generations-old conception voiced by Thomas Jefferson.

He was aware that much of the enormous reservation given to the Sioux, taking up most of the western Dakotas, had been retaken (a model for the ugly custom called "Indian giving," he supposed) and returned to the public domain and re-opened to settlement, giving the Indians in return nothing but more white neighbors and drastically diminished resources. He assumed, as many did, that the unannounced overall plan was intended to further impoverish the individual Indians who were given title to pitifully small parts of the remaining reservation land, to the point where they would have to liquidate even these to survive. And meanwhile, the portions of land once set aside but not allotted were declared "surplus lands" and likewise opened to white settlement. Chessler felt always for his spiritual forebears and brothers, but had no meaningful way of protesting, any more than did the Sioux.

He learned through one of the travelers he met that a Dr. Bland, the Indian Assistance Association's president, from the East, after coming to Pine Ridge with the Secretary of the Interior's permission, was promptly banished and escorted off by then-superintendent McGilly Cuddy, with the blessing of the latter's informant, Senator Dawes. And of how Red Cloud, the head chief on the reservation, had offered to send a hundred braves to Gannoe's ranch not far away in Nebraska, where he was staying, to escort him back.

He, of course, did know that the young Lakota bucks had been permitted by Superintendent Brennan to slip into eastern Wyoming onto their old hunting grounds periodically for years, their presence upsetting townspeople and settlers and vexing lawmen. Who in eastern Wyoming could avoid knowing about that? But what was the harm, after so much real harm had been done to them? To Indian thinking, the whites must have had a demon to be so spiteful.

As for Martin, his thinking was colored deep crimson by hatred. The Indian's ways were those of vermin. The Indians were his mother's killers, and those who defended them were treacherous traitors to civilization.

Most of all, he hated and feared Red Cloud, a man then in his eighties, certain that if the remnants of the plains hordes that annihilated Custer and now gathered there be in any way judged sufficient, they were bound to be put back together and hurled at the defenseless settlements where the red man's grazing and gathering empire had so lately been. And as heedless as were the soft and forgetful new settlement generation who had merely inherited the land so fiercely won, Red Cloud, or maybe his son Jack Red Cloud for him, would come as another Genghis Khan, sweeping away the mere mirage Martin knew was white civilized power on the ground and put the survivors of its onslaught to flight.

He even suspected that the Lakota's fawning Pine Ridge agent, his sworn enemy Brennan, who had once thrown him out of Rapid City, might himself lead or abet the onslaught, following the wishes of the naïve and soft-headed Indian Assistance Association in the East. And then, at last, he, Martin, well backed up by the Wyoming Volunteer Regiment, would exact his sweet and proper revenge and watch them die slowly from an overlooking ridge and smile in remembrance of his great friend and fellow Colonel, Custer.

Martin remembered how he and Custer and Calamity Jane had cavorted together in a horse race and shooting match and drained draws together at the Mud Flat Saloon in Bear Camp, on the exact spot where Rapid City would arise, in the dawn days of the Black Hills. At that time, he reminded himself over and over, Brennan, a Major in his own mind only, was still peddling flowers back east somewhere. He would yet see the eyes of that phony, and that egg-sucking dog Red Cloud's, sightless gaze into space. And not to forget the spawn of the first loathsome Old Chessler, waiting now in full submission in Martin's own back yard, kept on the fringes of his very own town, as insolent and Indian-coddling as his whore of a pa back at Fort William before it was proper Laramie. And no more fit to breathe than the Churches had been. Lost in reverie, Martin drained his whiskey down nightly and smoked his war pipe.

◄►

Chief Red Cloud, the greatest living Oglala Lakota, was not unanimously proclaimed as such by the coming generation. Among them, and present among those who now approached him to request a travel pass to head west for a hunt that fall, were some who knew that he fought off the whites more valiantly and to better effect than any other chief since Little Bighorn. And there were those who knew that, unconquered in battle, he lost his fight and acquiesced to his people's crushing subjugation. The former called him supreme, and the latter *fofo*—soft, or even senile.

Sensitive and shamed by the disrespect of the latter, the almost 82-year-old received the young delegation in his lodge by facing away, his back toward them, his replies to their entreaties so soft-spoken they had to strain to hear.

"You told our fathers before Wounded Knee that there would be buffalo again and the white man gone," Eagle Feather, a proponent of Red Cloud, addressed him for those he wouldn't hear, so as not to embarrass him by their taunts.

"Ah, yes, the solace of the Ghost Dance."

"Now we want to go and see if it is as you have spoken."

"You must accept the reality of that which you can see yourself."

"Will we find buffalo?"

"Seeking them is something that will be rewarded."

"Why did you believe in the power of Ghost Dance?"

"Because the buffalo returning would mean we can decide matters for ourselves without leave of anyone." He paused and then went on. "With the superintendents or agents, everything depends on whether the Republicans or Democrats are in power. There are two minds, and whichever comes to control removes the agent sent by the other and reverses the policy. Under Cleveland, one group of chiefs was favored and the other disfavored. The order is now the other way. The Oglala are without power. If you see the buffalo in the west, our strength will return."

It was understood that the subject of their request was not to be raised. Red Cloud would advise Brennan, when asked, precisely as Red Cloud would advise.

◄►

Having two names, Indian and white, was a common reminder at Pine Ridge of the slow but steady disappearance of the red race. And who were the double-named individuals? Were they, in the main, products of stable unions marked by mutual respect and kindly affections? No, they were often no more than inevitable results of liaisons of convenience, expressions that men needed to lie with women, even if those of their own kind were not conveniently available. And, equally, that native women were attracted by glittering, cheap jewelry, attire, and flimflam they couldn't otherwise have hoped to obtain. Indirect fruits of lust they were—of the flesh and of the eyes! And the Indian side of the frontier became alive and littered with the likes of Eagle Feather/Charlie Smith and a thousand fellows who hated their tandem names, and could never live on either side of the racial divide without stigma and suspicion. And a little shunning leads, frequently, straight to fanaticism: to their out-Indianing other Indians.

But Eagle Feather/Charlie Smith was different from most. Because of superior native intelligence, as well as extra drive—what white ethnologists or eugenicists might have rather libelously labeled "hybrid vigor," he was a natural leader of young half-breeds and malcontents.

And there was more than just the white genetic material to blame for his misfortune of being "mixed up." There was also the increasing prevalence of pale-faces among his neighbors on the joke of a reservation—barren land with little game, assigned precisely because that's what it was. But the land, nevertheless, even lying as it did between the fabled Sand Hills and the famous Badlands, did grow some grass in places, and so could support some white man's cattle, now that the buffalo were wiped out.

And so, white men naturally wanted the land back. And allotments meant that no tribe collectively owned it anymore, but only individual Indians owned each one lot, parcel, an "allotment" of land. Not enough land to scratch a living from, though, if they even knew how to do that. And so, receiving less than enough supplementary rations to boot, they frequently found themselves forced to sell out to available buyers (non-Indians, since Sioux Indians didn't have any money), in order to keep body and soul together. And so, more of the neighbors every year were white, as well as more in the towns that were white.

And the law was white, which required promising young Sioux, even part-Sioux, like Eagle Feather, to go to white man's Indian indoctrination school far away to learn white man's learning, white man's religion, white man's ways, and the utter worthlessness of following backward Indian ways. Charlie was an alumnus of Carlisle, but not a convinced alumnus.

For instance, he regarded the history he learned there as a lie, as it pertained to the Plains Wars and the virtue of one civilization robbing and disinheriting and taking prisoner the other.

Charlie despised white men, though not as individuals. Some of his white neighbors were pleasant and neighborly, and he believed that some among them might even defend him and his family, share food and give shelter in case of an emergency or attack. But he despised the white civilization for its built-in air and assumption of superiority, mistaking numbers for worth. Just as his civilization couldn't survive after the white man had destroyed the buffalo, the white civilization couldn't survive ultimately, and would have to retreat, if somehow the grazing land and the farm land it depended upon were destroyed or failed. He often thought about this, and the meanness of the deliberate destruction of the Indians' food source and sacred animal, and then dividing and re-conquering the Indian with the allotment to get back even the worst land that had been relegated for his use. And he learned also at Carlisle of the trick deceitfully called "Indian giving." *How unspeakably wicked!*

◄►

Because of its non-strategic location on his lower right calf, Chessler's suppurating deep sore, even while showing signs of infection, didn't slow him or prevent him from any task he needed to undertake. But it did all but paralyze him with worry at times. What was to become of him, and what would become of Daniel without him? How could be convert the treasure he had found to secure the boy's future without attracting attention? And how was he to care for himself without outside aid when debilitated by the inevitability of a spreading infection?

At times, particularly at night, the pain—especially, the mental pain—had already become difficult to bear, and it worried him to think what it might be like in the months ahead. But to share his mounting distress with Daniel was perfectly needless—for, what could the boy do that he couldn't for himself, except duplicate his worry and his deep-felt frustration with the unjust stupidity—Martin's and perhaps his own—preventing him from securing appropriate attention?

He thought back on his boyhood and what his surrogate moms, the Lakota women, might have done to sooth and heal such a wound. Luella Church, he was sure, would have known about that better than he. He imagined the remedy would have involved snakeroot, chewed and directly applied. But snakeroot, if he could even recognize it now, wouldn't appear for another month, past when all of the snow had gone.

In the meantime, he thought to try and convert the feed shed (fittingly, the probable location of the inception of the wound) into a sort of sweat lodge. And for that he could enlist Daniel's help, for making a sort of health island or resort on their property, as some might call it.

So, he thought to put in extra, upward-angled louvers in the upper walls as vents, and fashion a large general fan from barn slats attached to a stake that could be grandly and slowly waved by one and then the other of them. And he converted the smaller iron stock tank part-time into a cauldron, where dampened hay and sagebrush branches could be scorched on top of smoldering wood to fill the concentrated space with plenty of steam. And the exposed skin of one and then the other of them could be quickened by smart flailing with willow branches. And maybe, in combination with the application of pungent aromatic salve, that could do some good toward healing, as he knew the Lakota swore by it. At least until the healing herbs should appear a little more into the spring.

But once all was ready, the materials ignited filled the little stock shed full of so much acrid smoke that he and Daniel had to run out half-naked, coughing and sputtering and yes, laughing (really, the best medicine) into the sweet cold air, ending the experiment. Perhaps tellingly, their dog Red was waiting just outside, to merrily run after them when they came running out, having, most unlike himself, refrained from entering. And the horses neighed.

The President was coming! The "Cowboy President" TR! And Newcastle town was agog—none more so than the Miller household, especially the Miller girls, and especially eleven-year-old Mary and nine-year-old Hellen, two of a half-dozen or so girls from the school chosen to strew wild flowers all up and down the President's path from the train station down to the special platform to be set up from which he was to address the crowd. And what a crowd was expected! Practically speaking, everybody in Weston County, probably Campbell County, and all around would be there—the biggest crowd ever in the good, broad, open and rolling county, the friendliest in Wyoming, for sure. The sheriff's wife, Anna—on the committee to decorate the platform in 45-star flag bunting (Wyoming being the newest of the states in the Union till then, save Utah)—was swept up as well, and insisted that her husband go down with her to Taylor's Store on Saturday to pick out a befitting new dark blue suit for the occasion.

Sheriff Miller was to be up on that platform himself, right alongside the President and Congressman Mondell and the Mayor providing security for the whole event. And Anna had never been as proud of her lawman husband or seen him as proud. The family quarters, in an apartment annexed to a jail, may have left something to be desired, but the happiness there had become almost complete, and what was lacking in the family's living space could be addressed later. She was working on it.

◄►

On a miserable rainy Thursday when he was almost seized up by the pain of his festering leg, Chessler moved on foot eastward through the backstreets of the town to carry out his resolution to confront "Slim" Clifton in his cell before the possibility expired altogether. It was an act of loyalty toward tragically extinguished friends. He had to find out whatever scraps of information he could to try to make some sense of the crime, at least for him.

Approaching the Court House and the jail, he beheld an unexpected minor hubbub. He watched helplessly as a horse-drawn cab with the curtains drawn rolled by, the unmistakable figure of Slim, bound and blindfolded, clearly visible for a brief instant looking in from the front of the vehicle, escorted by a small retinue led on horseback by Deputy Owens, the ex-Sheriff. Being an old hand, and from hearing talk at his saloon, the consummate man of action, the deputy, had divined there was a plot afoot.

In all of the excitement of the President coming, Sheriff Miller had almost forgotten to order the temporary transfer of the prisoner across to Custer, in Dakota, for safekeeping.

Now old Chessler felt an extra burden, as if he had let his friends down by waiting too long to come on his dreaded errand, as irrational and perhaps self-pitying as that thought actually was.

And Martin, as it happened, was watching, too, in silence from under the dripping green and white striped awning of the Antlers Hotel down the street. Watching and pondering.

Slim himself had simply passed into numbness from sleeplessness, gloom, and a blue smolder of stabbing fear. Choking on big silent sobs others didn't detect, his hands were rope-burned, being drawn too tight behind him, and his posterior cold on the hard leather slab of the seat. There was no balm in Gilead, or from any other known quarter.

10

THINGS PORTENTOUS

Unprecedented, *unheard of* throngs of locals from America's close-to-last frontier were standing, milling, beside themselves with anticipation awaiting the progression from the train platform to the speaking platform of the cowboy-hero President who came, in a sense, from their own back yard—*unmistakably, one of them!* A small handful of recent local veterans who had come out to the Wild West after their glorious service in the Spanish-American War and a few among them who rode with the Roughriders were there. And a great many more who remembered having ridden with a peculiar near-sighted, scholarly wrangler and stock owner called "Four Eyes" throughout the region, or at least said they did, were also in attendance, anticipating, perhaps, at least a toothsome smile and a wave of recognition.

Uncharacteristically, Martin was not known to have spread any stupendous stories of days and nights on the trail with Roosevelt, nor was he conspicuously in attendance at the lectern or even at the awaited event. A rumor passed through some of the crowd about his health. Chessler, from a longer perspective, privately suspected that he couldn't reconcile not being the president himself, and couldn't stand being upstaged beyond all comparison, particularly by someone he might have once ridiculed, and who might even remember.

But those who were in attendance were in an ecstatic mood. On that memorable Saturday, all of Weston County was ablaze with excitement and pride. TR was, enthusiastically, one of their own. And one of their own he was—even though he came from another, older and refined part of the country, he belonged to them because he had chosen to come and live their life among them. He knew what they knew of the tough frontier world now passing, and proved himself worthy as few silver-spooners ever had. And succeeding here as well as *there* had made it damn near certain, at least in their eyes, that he could rise to the office of President of the United States, *or just about anything else.*

When that appointed Saturday came, *everybody* showed up. Virtually everybody did, at any rate. An immense throng of two-thousand people, four hundred or so from Cambria, the older coal-mining center, and some from farther, even South Dakota—the biggest crowd ever in the little community's short history. And all the streets were filled with horses, carriages and rigs, leaving something of a nightmare clear-up problem behind for the city crew.

What a glorious spring day was that Saturday in Newcastle—a balmy 70 degrees, cloudless blue sky and just a puff of a breeze. Daniel was present for sure, to commemorate his patriotic heritage and witness history, along with Chessler, suffering silently with his throbbing leg, trying to withhold it from any possible jostling out on the rim of the throng, but still with a clear view of the unmistakable great warrior as he trundled up the steps and onto the platform just like a bow-legged old cowpoke, the homely sight of which provoked an involuntary chuckle from Chessler.

He, for one, had never seen a president before. And he suspected that many or most of the dozens who braggingly reminisced around the town never had, either. Still, a privileged few of them must have experienced him close-up for real. And how strange and humbled they must have felt.

The mayor and sheriff proudly greeted the President, arriving precisely on time at 11:30, hale and happy, both dressed in the ubiquitous dark suit of the day accompanied by Wyoming Congressman Mondell of Newcastle. The acting governor of the state, Republican De Forrest Richards, had been too ill to make the trip.

Especially for long-time area residents, it seemed almost as if he had traveled from his Dakota ranch up the line and just popped into Newcastle, right on the sundown side of the Black Hills, for a visit or perhaps on some routine business. *One of them* as President of the United States? Even seeing him *in the flesh*, that did seem a stretch! And, he certainly could not have been totally unaware of the irony his until recently unexpected appearance back here undoubtedly presented for some!

The schoolgirls who spread the flowers in the path of the procession to the dais, including the Miller daughters, and the Boys' Brigade drill team that marched along the way, couldn't have done the town and county—and, it seemed, the beaming President himself—more proud. Anna Miller had eyes only for her handsome and heroic husband up on the stage, seemingly lifted to a new height of virtue and honor as he stood tall and proud right next to the greatest and most recognized man in the world. So fixed and guileless was her gaze that a fly could have flown between her open lips.

And then, the great one in their midst was speaking, a once-in-a-century paradox: the great from afar among the mundane – *this* mundane. The President first expressed his gratitude, mentioning especially the singularity of the flowers that were strewn! Then, he recounted his personal familiarity with the area, gained on a ride in with a string of horses nineteen years earlier, and mentioning the Belle Fourche, Powder River, the Tongue, and the Rosebud range as places he knew. He saluted the new State's base of ranching, farming, and mining as propitious and salubrious, and lauded the spirit of hard work, honesty, integrity, and intelligence he saw as exemplified by the older pioneers and the new generation of Wyoming as fundamental to the nation's strength and purpose.

The President pointedly denounced the maintenance, practice, and presence of *fear*, and declaimed forcefully that such had no legitimate place in the governing of the country. (In other words, *the only thing to be feared is fear.*)

But, what he refrained from including in his remarks—the salute many expected to the great part played by the soldiery in conquering and defending the western land—must have given the veterans present from the late foreign war and the not long ago Indian campaigns some cause for disappointment.

His speech concluded, he departed with his small retinue for the waiting train, his progress this time accompanied by the town's concert band. Before leaving to continue on to Yellowstone, he greeted and, from the platform, shook the hand of everyone who could reach him.

And then, a very strange and sinister thing happened. No sooner had the presidential "Square Deal Express" pulled away, belching and steaming, as the crowds of onlookers dispersed back to where they came from, than the guards returning the notorious prisoner, shielded from view by the drawn curtains of the special phaeton dispatched for the trip, pulled up behind the jail. And, as soon as darkness began to cloak the gusty, red-sky dusk, a different tempered crowd came striding, as if automatically, six and eight abreast, approaching fast up the street. A loud fracas soon blew up outside the jail, and on the exact stroke of nightfall, a torch was lit and waved high overhead by one of the leaders of the exceedingly agitated assemblage.

As Deputy Owens showed up and walked toward the jailhouse steps in the midst of the hubbub, the sudden crowd parted and quieted, allowing him through. The town's de facto two sheriffs, standing together there on the steps, seemed some-what taken aback. Gravely surveying the gathering, they in fact recognized only a small number as for a certainty local men. And there was a single brave, tall woman standing out among them in the front row.

"Now, just let us handle this!" Billy Miller, the actual sheriff, still in his special dark tailored suit, spoke plaintively into the temporary hush. "You fellas, and ma'am, return to your homes, please. Our friend inside, Mr. Clifton, is owed a trial, the same as anyone in similar circumstances would be." Miller's well known horse, Surprise, a gift from the admiring mine manager Kendrick, was tethered and pawing the ground next to the concrete steps into the building.

"That's right, men," Johnny Owens concurred, flicking the barrel of his out-sized Colt 50 along his smooth-shaven chin. "We mean to protect the prisoner and see that justice is served."

A murmur of dissent spread through the mob, rose and flourished and died down after a full two minutes. Then, there came a voice from back inside the throng that Owens thought sounded like the locksmith Bailey: "What if he gets that lawyer, Standley, from Lusk, that got that rogue Rodgers off last year?"

"Yeah," another man shouted, "and what if they gits to be a woman, or *women* on the jury? Why, he could git him clean off!"

"Not in *our* community!" a voice from clear in the back sounded, and the crowd concurred.

"Why, you wouldn't want this jail, your home, with your woman and all the young-uns inside, burned down!" the apparent Bailey figure, with little Ed right up beside him, judging from his profile in the dark, spoke for all, and they all shouted their approval.

Owens and Miller conferred and the man at the front waved his torch wildly, sparks cascading in the direction of the door.

Within a few more minutes, the service door at the side swung open, and Slim Clifton, dressed in little, dashed out and ran across the street, disappearing in the dark amidst some bushes. Whether he somehow sprung himself, was sprung by someone in the assembled mob, or was released to avoid the more serious disaster threatened, was hard to say.

But the crowd moved forward as one, crossing over to literally beat the bushes for him. The sound of un-raked old leaves being tramped went on for a good ten minutes and receded as the pursuers moved systematically into the interior of the spacious yard of one of the community's larger homes. Finally, there was what sounded like a colossal crash of some kind and some more loud yelling, and they emerged back toward the darkened street, bearing the intended quarry upside down, held by one leg and one arm.

Anna Miller, listening intently through the window of her residence, thought she heard him scream like a captured rabbit. She turned out the lights inside.

And then, the whole throng, every single one of them, drifted fast, still bearing the prisoner, down toward the high wagon bridge over the tracks, as the two lawmen, seeming beside themselves, paced and dithered on the doorstep of the manse. "I'll pick my fights," someone thought they heard John Owens remark. Others disputed that.

Moonlight shined clearly on the unanimated faces of the suddenly-sobering and fast-scattering beholding mob as the loudly groaning , then muted man, neck-laced far too snugly by the hanging rope, dropped extremely violently, and fast. The man's head popped upward, leaving the body, and fell with a sickening flat thump onto the rock pavement a distance below, as both genders emitted distinctive gasps of terror. It seemed a wonder, but practically none present were recognized. And no one was criminally charged.

◄►

A question raised in the end by surprisingly few of the attendees at the address downtown by President Roosevelt was, where on earth was Martin, the close-to-exclusive owner of the town and county, on such a day as this? Most probably, most in attendance didn't give the lack of even so much as a mention of him from the stage, let alone his physical absence, a thought. But then, there was the stock answer that circulated among those who did note his absence, that he had been called out of town on some pressing piece of business. Chessler thought about it, and supposed that that very vague rumor had probably been spread by the tumultuous old strongman's associates, who likely didn't know where he was, either.

In fact, he had arrived, unannounced and dead drunk, at the door of the immaculate, fairly spacious apartment of his daughter-in-law, Iris, and gotten detained by business there. Iris was the widow of his deceased son Thomas, and her apartment was above Taylor's Store, heavily mortgaged to Martin's bank.

Iris was a nurse at the hospital, an outspoken advocate of civic improvement and amenities, though impeded somewhat in this by her family. She came from an honest, rough-hewn family in Crook County, farther north, and had grown up a neighbor and friend of Anna, the wife of Sheriff Miller.

Thomas, Martin's good son, and Iris had not had children, but Iris regarded her precocious niece Penny, Daniel's school friend, as the daughter she never had.

Indeed, Penny seemed much more fittingly the progeny of Thomas and Iris rather than vile Manfred and shrewish Helen, and in fact clung with loyalty and affinity to her aunt and regarded her as her model.

Penny's little sister, Martina, was, by contrast, short and dark, and looked and acted more like her two parents, and had been likened more than once to a *poltergeist,* as volcanic and difficult as she was. Iris remained in Newcastle solely, by all appearances, to do her best to stabilize the raucous family—a thankless job.

Iris was excited about attending the President's once-in-a-lifetime appearance with her niece, Penny, and planning to meet her in an hour when Martin arrived. She felt the bottom drop out of her stomach when she realized who was at the door and in what condition.

There had been a time, shortly after the unsolved murder of her husband, when she had felt soft-heartedly indulgent to this now shell of a man, Martin. Her foreboding father-in-law had often been charming and generous toward her during her marriage, and she felt he had suffered enough with the loss of one of his twin sons and the virtual idiocy of the other, as well as the early senility of his wife Esther, who still spent endless days rocking idle and forgotten in the attic of their large home.

Now, Iris tried for what must have been the hundredth time to hold the old dog at bay, her sympathies, she now realized belatedly, having been misunderstood. The oft-repeated scene, though no one outside had ever witnessed or heard of it, was invariably the same.

Holding him back was like holding back a muscular and determined two-hundred-pound nine-year-old. He pushed and groped her, calling her the "spittin' image" of his sainted mother. He praised her during his assault for her beauty, grace, and "smarts", for how she had redeemed her lowly and busted-luck family. And he slowly ripped another of her dresses to tatters—she was constantly mending them. He would not hear to "no" because, as he said, he was a lonely and harmless old man, and she was lonely and, despite her denials, in need of warmth and a little affection for all the sacrifices they both had made for their family.

And he inserted his usual trump card of mentioning her inheritance. And when she reminded him yet again that she didn't care anything about that, he threatened to cut off Penny's inheritance if she ever left town, and throw himself headlong into the Belle Fourche River rapids that day if she eluded him—more credible.

Inevitably, her strength would fail after an hour of struggle, and she would fall back as always upon her surest line of ultimate, if costly, safety. She knew with certainty that he would bully her backward onto her bed and humiliatingly strip her of her underwear, but from that point, be entirely useless, innocuous as far as fathering or entering, and it let her breathe a little.

11
SMITHEREENS

Iris was left feeling torn nonetheless—seared by flashbacks and bruising, by tattering of her garments and person. How could such an old, muddled man attack her, and then flat-out rant, "We will socking right show those butchers again?" she pondered, and "'We will butcher *them* every one, just as we did once—women, children, men, all nits and lice alike, to protect YOU again, Helen. Just like last year...'" Last year? 1902? Protect you? What? Protect you, Helen like last year? Nits, lice?

Humiliated, breathless, and sobbing. Bruised. Not penetrated anymore, but seared by his fiery alcohol breath and saliva, face-down, smoldering. She'd missed the event of the century, for *that!*

Poor Penny—what could she tell her? Tears no longer were even a response. She was *letting* him. *LETTING* him!

◄►

TR, as he sped along in the rail coach, thought back on what an ideal and peaceful and wonderful little city Newcastle was; just the sort of place he might like to move to himself—at least part of him would—if he could.

◄►

Martin, alone that evening but for the senile old woman upstairs, in his big old house on Wolcott Street, scrawled in his diary: "Stopped by today and saw to welfare & needs of my good daughter-in-law Iris. Assisted as I could. Happy to find her apt. well-kept and person attentive & bright, as usual. Her recovery remarkable. Visited & swapped yarns with old trail companion, Roosevelt, in town for day. Sunny and windy."

◄►

Chessler finally had to get a grip on himself. He walked all the way from the top of Main Street out to beyond the west end, where the last dirt street ended in the dust and sagebrush, to where his low little hovel built by now-forgotten pioneers stood. His misery in suffering the continuing anguish from his untreated and un-healing wound must not extend to Daniel or be permitted to compromise his future. He was indeed fortunate, he kept thinking, to have at his disposal a secret source of unexpected bounty for the boy's future. On their slog back home, he resolved to take the fullest possible advantage of the good spring weather and all of the strength he still possessed to lay by treasure.

"What did you think of the President, son?" he inquired.

"I thought he had more energy, more fire in him, than any man I ever seen— even than most ten, I reckon," came the adolescent's unexpectedly thoughtful reply. "As an example for us, there could hardly be an equal. Did he really live out here in this county once?"

"Yes, and not that many years ago. He rode into Wyoming on a horse, leading horses, back then, as he said. A far sight from where he is now, wouldn't you say?"

"Yes. But he's learned from what we do have here, and what we think of as good. And it's like we're there in that place he's in with him. He's proud still to be a westerner. You could tell!"

"Yeah! You're right!" the proud older western plainsman agreed. "It seems like he's learned from us—our land and the good people that's here, and now, today for instance, he has sort of give back to us. So's we could feel proud! It's almost like Newcastle was his town. You could feel that in the way he spoke. He let us feel real good about who we are out here, sort of pioneers still, in a way."

Daniel thought, but didn't say, how it was odd that his Pa, of all people, could still say that, with the way he was treated by the town.

And Chessler, feeling the juicy, stinging ooze under his rude wrappings, wondered again to himself how it would ever all stop. And he resolved to get to work.

◄►

Come Sunday afternoon, the next day, right after their repast of corn beef gruel, old Chessler pronounced, "We must make hay while the sun shines!" He and Daniel and Red then arose directly and, hitching up Lanie and Jerry, drove their lurching, rickety old buckboard around on the rough road past the south side of Newcastle, over to their water station on the sloping plain above the creek beside the stage road. Because, Daniel knew he didn't really mean hay.

And as usual, Chessler harnessed himself with the staked rope and backed himself down into the precipice onto the jumble of rocks on the stream bed of Salt Creek, still gurgling along from spring snow-melt, with Daniel posted, as usual, as sentinel. Employing the grasping, long-handled iron hook he had fashioned, the prematurely fast-aging codger then extended it down into a deep crack between rocks to try and coax another of the shining long bricks in sight—each weighing 27.5 lbs.—upward so he could take it up the rope and stash it under the floor of the ruined chicken coop next to the cabin. It was excruciatingly hard work, but it had to be done.

Daniel sometimes begged to be the one to descend and bring up the ungainly prize now, but Chessler was reluctant to expose his boy to the rigors of it and the danger of falling to the bottom, at least while he himself was able.

But Daniel's part in the enterprise, though not as arduous, was nearly as important. He had to pay attention and listen very attentively to warn his pa early to return at once to the decrepit water house if anyone was coming. Chessler's hearing was no longer keen enough to hear travelers on the road approaching while working before they were in sight. And for his part, Red had to be trained not to bark when requested.

When engaged in transferring the gold, the hastily-ditched booty from what was now a decades-earlier heist, Chessler's memory often returned to that once-in-a-lifetime kind of a day years ago when he'd seen John Owens at his roadhouse down in the shadow of old Fort Laramie remove his apron and put it on the guard who'd just stepped off the stage. For whatever reason, Johnny had never, it would seem, completely unraveled the mystery from that day. And no one else ever did, either.

They brought up four bricks from the canyon before the end of the day, with no company or water-buyers arriving until just half an hour was left till sundown. And then it was Alexander Antioch, the old-time tinker-merchant, peddling a few items Daniel could never see why anyone would want—a well-used bed spring, a warped washboard, chipped pottery, some sort of antique water clock—approaching in his made-over covered wagon. Daniel gave his shrill whistle, and Pa came scrambling out, busting down and stumbling through the brush, and arrived just seconds before old man Antioch rolled to a stop.

"Waa, whot's this, man?" the puny, sharp-nosed intruder, draped nearly to his knees in hanging white hair, inquired mysteriously in his piercing alto. "An, whacha doin' a-warkin' on the Sabbath, thar, boy?"

Daniel was unclear as to whether himself or Chessler was being referred to.

"Ya don' see me a-warkin," old A.D. Antioch continued. "No, Sar! Jist a crusin' up to town for the marnin' tamarra, thet's all!"

Daniel pumped him a tin cup of water before he could even ask, and set about at once to provide a bucket for this wayfarer's donkeys.

Chessler leaned his weary frame against the ramshackle frame of what had once been a genuine building and wiped the sweat of his brow on his frayed and hanging shirtsleeve and sighed deeply.

"Whatcha been doin'?" asked Antioch shrilly. "Warkin', was ya? On the Sabbath! Man, you walkin' on the edge!"

Chessler never could decide whether the man was serious in these admonishments, and made the mistake of grinning and chuckling and shaking his head.

Old Antioch looked as stunned as if he'd been slapped, his watery blue eyes gazing with profound solemnity. Could he actually be blind and still travel around with his donkeys to all the old places after so many years? Daniel wondered, his mouth open a little.

But the old fellow didn't stay around very long this time, no doubt wanting to get on toward town while at least his donkeys could see.

And he had no more than left the proprietors' sight before they packed up to head back themselves.

◄►

At school on Monday, heading into the end of the spring term, Daniel and his friend Penny Osgood each found the other unusually downcast, and each was concerned and wondered why. Penny intimated that she was worried about her beloved aunt, Iris, who didn't show up as planned to meet President Roosevelt—which was not like her at all. And when she saw her at church on Sunday morning, she claimed she simply had not felt well on Saturday. Iris had never let her down like that before.

When Penny inquired as to why Daniel did not seem himself, he was reluctant to answer, because he didn't like to discuss his circumstances at home. But she wouldn't relent, and finally he admitted his father had an untreated and worsening severe wound on the calf of his right leg, that was vexing him and threatening to destroy his leg or even his life.

Daniel had hesitated to tell her in part because he feared Penny might know about his pa's being spurned for a supposed offense against community values, by what amounted to an order from her grandfather, and not be sympathetic. But he was mistaken.

"Oh, Daniel," she said, "I am so sorry to learn that. I wish there was something I could do for you!"

"I wish there was, too," he found himself saying, and the smile they shared cemented their friendship.

◄►

Bobby Gammage, the editor of the *News-Tribune*, started to write up the report of Diamond Slim's sad end at the hands of strangers on Sunday night. Too bad this fine little city turned its best day ever into one of its worst so quickly, he thought. Then, Carmen, his loving and lovely wife of two years, came in and leaned over his shoulder to read what he was writing. Surprisingly, she clicked her tongue, and in an inimitably low, mannish voice, pronounced, "No, dear. Do you want them to pounce on my supposed past even now?"

Hearing this, Gammage inhaled deeply and summarily wadded up the writing paper and chucked it in the trash. And then they stood and embraced tightly and warmly. "A dance hall girl you was," he cooed, "but not now." Then he sort of mumbled aside to himself, "Besides, to me, yellow skunk lyin' and murderin' might be worse."

◄►

Anna Miller felt discouraged and deflated come Sunday night after her husband had turned icy cold and taciturn, so soon after being the brightest and proudest—the *happiest*—she had seen him in years. She told him what happened Saturday night had not been his fault, but he wouldn't hear it. He had lost the prisoner without securing trial, and that was that.

Her one ray of sunlight was a plan to involve him, so dashing in his new suit, in attending at least one night of the traveling Chicago Opera Company's performance a week hence of "Marriage of Figaro" at the Newcastle Opera Hall. Maybe that would help pull him out of the doldrums.

And to think, what a profile their little city was making as it grew up, she reflected. Twentieth century, indeed! What happened Saturday night would soon be forgotten, the last act of the old brutality and nastiness. And she didn't like to think of such a thing; the words could never have been dragged out of her. But she had to admit, to herself, at least—the man probably had deserved little better.

◄►

A mystery that plagued Johnny Owens that Sunday night and in the early hours of Monday, forsaken and forlorn on his little ranch, way out by the ruins of old Tubb Town, was: who unbolted that door? It was not the first or last time John Owens had lost a man or failed to command a situation. But it galled him, and it would for a good while, though even an inferno of fire wouldn't have stopped that committee of vigilance from surging in pursuit and having its way. But who in heaven's name had either left that door deliberately unlocked, or picked that special, deluxe, two-hundred-dollar double bolt lock that he had had installed himself?

Assuming the presumed lock-pick was from Newcastle, there was only one man in town who might have been able to do that, leastwise as quickly as it would have had to been done, if that's what happened—Bailey, the jeweler. Who was one of Martin's mob. Because he had seen him coming out of Antlers with them after a spree. And, he'd discussed it with Joe LeFors, and Joe had been of the same opinion—not discounting that one of the number spotted in the crowd that night from Converse or Crook County might have been able to do it.

He was thinking he would go back into town tomorrow and try to lift some fingerprints from the door, on his own—Miller wouldn't even have to know it, something very easy to accomplish if you just knew when he braked to eat.

He couldn't even discount that Miller might have been in on it. He couldn't discount anything. But it would have done him no good, certainly, to voice his suspicions.

◀▶

And then there was Slim Diamond L. Clifton, his last, futile, friend being protective John Owens, keeping his own counsel still, denied due process, stuffed in a hole. *Until last call.*

12

GREAT PLAINS GRAND OPERA

After four days of in effect silence as somber as if there the death had been in the family, Anna Miller came slipped back in Wednesday evening straight from her weekly quilting bee with her circle of ladies, giggling to herself like a schoolgirl. So positively giddy she was that she finally managed to work a grin out of Billy, her man on whose lap she purposefully plopped as she hadn't in a good long time.

"What's this?" he asked, more than a little taken aback.

"Well," she started, chuckling while eyeing all the doors back into the apartment to make sure none of the children were coming just then. "I just heard—what would you say?—the darnedest thing. You know that Margaret, the piano player sometimes at the Antler, and sometimes at Johnny's place? The sort of a rough gal, but a good soul, really?"

"Yeah, of course I know—I mean, I know of her," Billy answered, always careful not to give the wrong impression, especially to his wife. "What? Has she gotten into some caper?"

Anna looked off into space, a kind of wistful look on her face. Then she laughed and shook her head. "It's the darnedest thing," she repeated. "Margaret, our Margaret, well, she's got herself a roommate at the boarding house, it seems." And the sheriff's schoolgirl wife's giggling started up again.

"Oh? Really?" her husband asked. "Anybody I would know about?"

"No!" she hooted. "You know, the Chicago Opera Company's coming into town, right?"

"Yeah. We're going to their play Saturday, aren't we?"

"Yes! We have a date! Well, anyway, they're coming in, and they tried to book at the Antlers Hotel, of course."

"Of course. Where else?"

"Well, the trouble is, the Wyoming Odd Fellows are having their convention here, too. And so, most of the rooms at the Antler were reserved to them."

"And so?"

"And so, a few of the members of the opera company were sent over to Carver's boarding house. And," she could hardly speak for guffawing at this, "that elegant opera diva..."

Billy Miller was afraid for a minute she might choke.

"...Chantelle Holiday, the world-famous soprano...has got our Margaret Dunning...good old country girl Margaret, for a roommate for the week. And I don't think they've met yet, but it's bound to be an absolute riot when they do!"

The sheriff just meditated on that vision of a first meeting for a minute, then it hit him, and he started to chuckle, too.

"I see what you mean," he said, returning to a mood a bit more somber, though likewise considering the contrast between the big-as-most-men, good-hearted, bluff, raw-boned, ruddy-complexioned unschooled local and the petite, refined, pale European blonde canary, amusing.

"When's she due in town?" Billy asked.

Anna burst into a laugh. "Tomorrow."

"How'd you find that out?" Billy asked.

"Verlana Howard, who works behind the desk there most days, gets off to attend the quilting circle. That Iris, Thomas's widow, used to come, but she quit." The sheriff's wife suddenly looked worried, and he wondered why she threw that in when she was talking about Margaret and the diva and things at Carver's boarding house, and spoiled a bit the all-too-rare happy mood.

When the train carrying the Chicago Opera Company rolled into town late the next morning, with a whole extra car to carry all the stage props and costumes, the stately looking men-actors strolled out onto the platform in their great coats and top hats and the ladies of the troupe in their frilly dresses and extravagant hats, the likes of which Newcastle had never seen. And people immediately started to take notice. These garments, coiffures, and ways of presentation were apt to set the fashion in the little city for a years to come.

Handlers sent out from the hotel and, in this case, Carver's boarding house, commandeered the luggage of each in carts and drove the arriving celebrities around in the hotel dray to find their respective accommodations and greet local dignitaries. Martin himself, overcoming his trademark shyness, waited to proudly stroll them over the short way to the resplendent new Newcastle Opera Hall, a product of the Weston County Foundation, of which he was the main patron. (Indeed, the new Hall, to replace one that had been destroyed by fire three years earlier, had been built quickly at the tyrant's insistence, to enable him to cut off Owens's theater venture from billing all the best companies and road acts into the town.)

The tour of the Opera Hall was not prolonged primarily because the members of the troupe were tired from their long trip and, in some cases, from more drinking and all-night card-playing and cigar smoke that they would have liked aboard the train, the Black Hills Zephyr.

Mme. Chantelle Holiday, in particular, the famous pint-size golden canary of the Chicago troupe, was more than glad to get out of confinement, claiming that all the cigar smoke strained her voice. So, she was anxious to be shown to her quarters for a rest.

And, in fact, Anna Miller would have found it comedic to watch her introduction to Margaret, the frankly profane but innocent woman piano player three times her size with whom she was to share a room for the next few days. Margaret, it turned out, was in the room when she arrived and couldn't have been any nicer or more hospitable, bending over and beaming to make the acquaintance of someone so petite, pretty, and at the same time, distinguished. And, to the astonishment of Clara, the proprietress, Chantelle was just as charmed and delighted with the plain, blunt woman's disarming sincerity and friendliness. The two of them became, in fact, instant friends.

But the little diva was also quick to note the tear coursing her new chum's cheek and a certain telltale redness in her eyes.

"Have you been crying, my dear?" she bravely ventured forth. "Whatever is the matter?"

"Oh, no, no! It's nothing!" Margaret fairly sobbed, smiling unconvincingly.

"Now," said Chantelle, looking up to her younger friend, "you must tell me, dear."

"Oh, oh…well. If you must know, I have a baby girl…at least, I *had* a baby girl. And they won't let me keep her."

"Won't let you keep her? Why not?"

"Because, I wasn't married. A man I met…a patron of the Antler, where I play the piano, well, he did me wrong."

"Your beau? Then, you have a beau?"

"Well, yes, I have a beau. But this man, he wasn't my beau, and…"

The pint-size diva looked very wise. "Oh…I see. But why can't you keep the little one?"

"Because," and she started sobbing, more lightly than before, again. "Because my boss...Martin, you met him. Well, he's a very important man. And some of the preachers in the town, and some of the church ladies, they went to Martin, according to what he said, and said I had to be punished for my errant ways. And so, they found a family to raise my baby. And, he said, Martin said, see...he wouldn't be able to employ me anymore if I kept her, because no one would come."

The diva, Miss Holiday, looked perplexed at this, then angry and then determined. Margaret thought it a wonder how her expressions changed as she digested what she'd heard.

Determined. That was what her uncompromising expression clearly said. "No," she spoke, pronouncing the word emphatically from low in her throat. "No. He can't tell you that! My dear, I must speak with this Mr. Martin...whatever his name is!"

"But," Margaret, flustered and feeling panic, protested. "But, you don't understand." She gripped the tiny woman's hand as she spoke. "He is a very important man. He owns almost everything around here, and—"

"No matter. He can't do that to you, and I must speak to him, now!"

Margaret was almost sobbing again, but this time from real fright. "But, he'll *fire* me!"

"He'll do no such thing! Now, where is he?"

Margaret bided her time, trying to think what to do.

Then, there came a gentle rap on the door, rescuing her momentarily. She opened the door slightly. "Oh, my handsome man!" she cooed, and Chantelle's and the eavesdropping char woman's ears pricked up. It was Alexander Antioch, the traveling merchant, a man half her size and twice her age, his white hair hanging down, and a rose in his hand.

"Do come in, darling," Margaret intoned. "And meet Chantelle Holiday, my new friend!"

"Playzed, Ma-am!" he offered, extending his sun-browned hand.

The diva took his hand gracefully in her small one, and he surprised everyone by leaning over and brushing her hand softly with his lips.

"But, I am going to speak to this...Mr. Martin, or whatever, if someone will show me exactly where he is."

The touch of European intonation in her inimitable voice could be counted on to command the attention of the more roughly-hewn.

Mr. Antioch, however, demurred. "You can count me out of *that*," he announced.

"Well, it doesn't matter, then. I'll have Mrs. Carver take me to him. She has promised to be at my disposal whilst here. Now, if you'll all excuse me..." With that, she turned abruptly, but somehow not dismissively, on her heel and moved back out into the lobby and over to where Mrs. Carver, the proprietress, was folding sheets brought freshly from the line.

The two odd lovers could then hear her voice echoing through the premises as she explained what she wanted to Clara Carver. And, looking out the door of the room, they saw the two of them vanish back out the entrance. No one, they learned, could stop this lady.

In ten minutes flat, she was back, beaming from ear to ear, to break the spell of apprehension that had gripped the room. "Your baby girl will be delivered right here to you within an hour," she announced.

Stunned, Margaret stood with her mouth open. "What? How?"

"I told him if he didn't do it, he would never get another troupe to come in and play his opera hall again. And I could arrange that!"

"But he'll *fire* me," Margaret, towering over both of the others, wailed.

"No, he won't. If he tries that, same thing, no more interest in his Opera Hall. It will flop like a wet noodle." Chantelle laughed. And they knew she was right.

Then, she turned briskly to unpack her luggage onto her assigned bed, as if she'd just arrived.

In a bit over an hour, baby Judy was back in Margaret's loving arms, and being doted over by the two new friends and even the old rascal with the long white hair, and cooing like nobody's business.

The fabulous new Opera Hall and the Chicago Opera Company and "Marriage of Figaro" were the talk of the town. The five hundred tickets available had sold out in three days, and Martin, who took the lead in raising up the new facility and bringing a world-class opera troupe to grace it, also benefitted from a good deal of favorable mention.

This, so close after the almost dreamlike visit from the President of the United States, and their lovely school, really a sort of palace of learning ensconced on the top of the hill overlooking all the town, were making Newcastle seem almost like a new Athens. So quickly, the ignominious epic of Diamond L. Slim and the benighted Churches was relegated to sometime in the bad old past. And Johnny Owens's house of entertainment was cast deep in shade by contrast.

Come Friday night, the forward part of the population—the society folks, as well as a lot of the plain folks who wanted in on the excitement—flocked through the door of the sprawling months-old Newcastle Opera House for its first really big entertainment, all clad in the most formal wear they owned. And some of the seats were filled by the reveling Odd Fellows convention folks, too.

Billy and Anna Miller sat in the center near the front, with the wide stage curtain stretching almost within their reach. The place filled in almost silently, polite low conversation only creating a sort of buzz that sounded a little like a hive of wasps while the ushered seating was continuing and the audience awaited the raising of the big, multi-colored curtain.

Then the long-awaited opera that was billed "Marriage of Figaro" with its dazzling song score, flashy costumed cast, brilliant scenery, and sharp-spoken dialogue, began. The whole of it struck like a shockwave, making the audience, every single one in the house, sit bolt upright in their cushioned seats, engaging everyone's attention as no show presented in that town—or perhaps anywhere in Wyoming—ever had. The residents took pride to learn that the Chicago Company was only to make its appearance that season in their own, bustling little metropolis of Newcastle and in the state capital, Cheyenne.

At the same time, there was a rumor that went around (as rumors do) that this Company was not really from Chicago, but merely a Nebraska troupe that had appropriated the name.

And, indeed, a murmuring had passed through the house, and not all present were content or remained, for some reason, enthusiastic throughout. At the end of the flawless performance, while most of the audience stood and applauded wildly, a few sections—some in which leading citizens were seated—withheld their approval and sat on their hands stone-faced until more than a few of the enthusiasts took note of their curious protest.

Curious until the man known as "Little Ed"—all 5'1" of him—stood boldly when the ovation of the enthusiasts had faded and ended, and shouted loudly the protesting verdict of the more than a few: "That was all of it in *Eye-talian*. Can't ya say it in Inglish? We hereabouts are Americans!"

And the few who were with him mumbled their rough approval.

The cast, completing its curtain call, stood like statues and stared, dumbfounded, and the curtain closed.

The show must go on the next night and, of course, would.

13

THE GRIM REAPER

Chessler and Daniel Edgemont were not able to attend the grand show in the new Opera Hall, because they couldn't be known to afford tickets. So they stayed home and experienced instead the light rain and engulfing mud that eventually marooned their lone dismal dugout, visible only from certain vantage points behind its hill, just past the edge of town.

Chessler nursed a slight fever and achiness, as he did increasingly these days, and was trying to read a newspaper in the dim glow of the low late-spring fire in the grate. Daniel struggled with his mathematics ciphers a couple of feet away, his mind habitually wandering to his recent days at school and conversations with Penny.

The gentle downpour wasn't letting up. A dozen jagged lightning bolts heading earthward at a time revealed a shining sea of rain-roiled shallow water extending down into the town, as far as a restive adolescent eye could see. Daniel watched Red, acting crazy in dark silhouette, out scrambling around, running nose-down, splashing and sending a jet off to one side, then the other, then back as he went. The two horses could be seen also silhouetted in the corral, running and rearing, spooked by the lightning and low rumbling behind it. And on the road, in the eastward distance, on the ridge coming up from town, he thought he could see a lone horse and carriage inching toward them. He continued watching the apparition emerge little by little from the watery mists until he was certain of it.

"Pa!" he announced, "I believe somebody's coming out this way."

"What? Who would it be, on a night like this, and with everyone in at the show?"

At precisely the same time, Daniel also began to notice the steady *drip! drip! drip!* of a leak from the ceiling in the southeast corner of their main room.

"Pa, I need the caulking gun! We got another leak in the roof, over above the stove!"

Chessler slowly unbent and stood up and, reaching down into his toolbox under the end of the table, handed his son the instrument for caulking leaks, which he applied standing on an old chair, staunching what was by then the start of a steady earthward river.

"Well, someone's pretty clearly on their way out here, at least starting up from the end of the lane," Daniel declared.

There was nothing more for it but to wait. They stood together and gazed out into the dark, and saw that the horse and carriage both appeared jet-black against the lightning-lit background of the sky. And the driver, too, emerged into view, a dark, hooded figure, reaching a slender or bony arm down to calm the nervous steed as they pulled up next to the almost-lightless hovel.

Chessler's head was still chockfull of stories of spirits and specters he had heard and retained from his boyhood half a century ago. And this aspect, combined with the touch of light-headedness he often felt, gave him a weird feeling about the conveyance and driver that had arrived out of the cosmic night. A hooded dark figure in what looked to be a spectral conveyance: Who in the solid and real world of earth could such a visitor be?

Then, in what seemed like no more than three or four seconds, there came a knock at the door that sounded just a little too loud and echoed hollow in the silence, save for the flow of water and the wind. Chessler hobbled over to the door, and could feel his leg sore throbbing and oozing alarmingly as he did.

He jerked the heavy door open a whole foot all at once and peered straight out into the eyes of a hooded personage—who he was surprised to find he recognized. Their mysterious visitor was, most unexpectedly, none other than the high and mighty Martin's daughter-in-law, Iris, whom they'd seen out on errands of her own and for the hospital of mercy on numerous occasions while down in the vicinity of central part of town. He noticed at once the look of resolve in her unblinking brown eyes, and the other thing he noticed right away was how slender and small she seemed inside that oversized dark-dyed hooded wool robe, apparently somehow almost perfectly rain-resistant.

"Mr. Chessler?" she inquired. "I am a nurse. I understand you have a dangerous leg wound and no recourse to treatment. I am bound by duty to allay your fear and bring needed help." For the first time, he noticed the sizable black leather case, about half as big as she, which she had borne in through the door behind her.

"You are an angel, and the extreme opposite of the kind I had feared from first appearances!" he remarked rather self-consciously. "You are, Ma'am, taking some kind of a risk for me!" A tear started to form in the corner of the poor man's now best eye.

She appeared to blush. "I am, yes, a little," she agreed. Though a rough cob he may have been in one sense, she thought, she was amazed to find him, after all she'd heard, at least an unusually well-spoken man. "I don't know what it was you were expecting, though," she said, cocking her head a bit to one side. "For this first time, at least, I waited until almost the whole town was detained. And, as it developed, the weather, as foul as it is, has aided my plan as well. I draped my carriage in black bunting before I left, to make it as inconspicuous and invisible as I could. And, of course, my horse is black, and virtually invisible in the night. I believe my vehicle, thus drawn, to most closely resemble a small hearse, or something of that order. But, seriously, I really doubt anyone at all saw me coming this way on this particular night."

"Coming here, of all places, in the dark of night..." he marveled and pondered, as if unable to quite fathom such a thing.

"Yes! My niece, Penny, pieced together, from what your Daniel told her"— here she blushed, spotting him standing near the fireplace, just daring to lift her eyes to the level of his—"what must be for you most cruel circumstances. And, it seems, all due to the prejudices of my father-in-law!"

"It's true, I'm afraid," Chessler allowed, sighing. "But a more capable man might be able to figure out how not to be so afflicted by it."

"But, you see," she remonstrated, "Martin is really not the powerful giant people seem to think of him as. Really, you see, he is weak and broken. No, he's not a whole man at all, at least now. And, let us agree, you and I, that we must not let him dictate our lives, either of us, any more to suit his foolish whims." He fancied he saw in the semi-darkness her lower lip quivering uncontrollably.

At least, both Chessler and Daniel were pleasantly shocked to learn that Martin's whole family, even aside from the willful Penny, were not arrayed against them, favoring Martin's view of things. Chessler had liked Thomas, Penny's husband, and spoke with him a time or two on business and in passing, but...

"But you're right," she said. "If he or Manfred catch me coming here, they could try to do anything. And, they do have eyes out and about in the night."

"Well, I'm very glad to see you've taken considerable precautions."

"Yes, certainly...though I'd best not tarry. The crowd will be moving outward from the Opera Hall and filling the streets soon."

He noticed she didn't delay her activity for a second while she talked. Opening her black case, she pulled out a roll of some indeterminate-looking material, a bottle of some liquid, a big tin of ointment, and an unusually long, wicked-looking pair of scissors, sending a little ripple of involuntary apprehension through the anxiously on-looking patient.

Chessler, at her bidding, rolled up his right pant leg, revealing the already badly soiled bandage and gauze wrapping he had just finished clothing the deep wound in, after cleaning it the best he could early that morning.

"It looks as if I've gotten here none too soon," she remarked, examining the dark, pus-filled lesion closely while daubing it ever so gently with an alcohol-soaked cloth, drawing an audible gasp from the normally stoic Chessler as he winced at her lightest brushing of the inflamed exposed nerve endings.

"You're fortunate to still have feelings there," she observed. "Have you been running a fever?"

"Yes, Ma'am, some...oh!"

"It's alright, Mr. Chessler. This must hurt a little bit. And I know you cannot stop your—*anybody's*—normal reaction. We must deal with it, though, if it is to heal."

"*Ahh!*" He genuinely felt relieved that she didn't consider him weak, but seemed to empathize. "Do you really think it can heal?"

"Yes, I think we can get it to heal. But we'll have to work with it regularly, change the dressings and clean it properly, and medicate it, at least twice a week."

"How do you know what to do with it?" Old Chessler asked, and, immediately feared that he had expressed doubt, which he didn't particularly feel, in her ability—or *anybody's*—to heal such a messy wound that wouldn't heal on its own.

"Well, I worked with a Dr. Haslit in Denver during a six months leave a couple of years ago, who had worked with a medical scientist named Paul Ehrlich, recognized as the 'father of antibiosis.' And he also pioneered the use of oiled silk—this material here," she indicated, lifting up the roll for him to see, "to wrap the wound so it will retain moisture and not scab, which, in a case like this, would block the tissue from receiving what it must."

Then, with her patient's mind on that bit of information—as quick as a cat— she took the sharp scissors and snipped away the sheen of dead tissue still adhering, causing a spark of sensation that his mind read as instant, intense pain, drawing a sudden pronounced "ouch!" from him, followed by a blush.

"Don't worry, it's okay," her voice soothed, even cooed, followed up closely by a fine, directed spray of bottled saline, and she worked in antibiotic lotion all around the edge of the round, open wound with her fingertips. Then, quickly, she re-wrapped the whole lower half of his leg in gauze and taped it loosely but securely. And then, suddenly, she was gone. To return in the evening on Monday or Tuesday, she said.

◄►

Down at the Antler later that night, Martin, Bailey, and the others were not in a jovial mood. "I warned you, Doc, that the name Opera Hall didn't mean you had to show real operas there," Jake the old rancher, from Big Beaver, reminded the unhappy boss.

"Ay, that you did," Martin allowed. "I didn't know it would be that sissy, lady stuff, men in frills, women like as that they sat on a water cushion, that kind of garbage."

"Whatever possessed you to?" Bailey inquired, now getting a little on Martin's nerves.

"I guess I must have been thinking of 'horse operas," he said. "I can see now why we didn't have a hard time booking them." The beer by now was flowing as fast as it ever did.

"You have to pay them the moon?" Little Ed asked.

"Naw, just the night's take of the house," Martin said. "And tomorrow night's. I have a half a notion to cancel it. 'Cept word would get around."

"Well," spoke a stranger in a deep baritone, decked out in fancy, tourist-style western gear with sequins and such, stepping boldly up to the informal council's perpetually reserved table in the back of the main room of the lounge. "I hope you won't cancel now. We went over really well with the ladies, and most of the real gentlemen—as we always do."

The whole table fell silent, all of its sour denizens taken aback by the male lead in the performance, the great baritone Philip Jerome—'Figaro' in the opera.

"Well, we...we..."

"Speaking French already?" Jerome joked. "You just aren't used to top-level entertainment in this neck of the woods, it seems," he said. "But if you're going to be part of this great country, you're going to have to learn to appreciate the sort of fare that New Yorkers and Philadelphians and, yes, Chicagoans are accustomed to and so enjoy. Just as they like your 'Buffalo Bill' and other Wild West shows. And, you're going to have to get over your fixation on fighting Indians and clearing this magnificent region of its bison—its natural cattle—just to introduce your own, which are really no better. Welcome to the twentieth century, gentlemen!"

The interloper raised the glass he was holding, and the men at the table, without any ardor, almost involuntarily, mostly by force of habit, raised theirs; but two down at the end registered their objections with groans.

"Beautiful town you have here—and congratulations on your lovely little opera hall. We'll find time to come back if you ever decide you want us." And he disappeared back into the veil of blue smoke in the dark among the tables.

◄►

Alexander Antioch, the old merchant-drummer, had stayed behind with the contented mother and was giving the baby its bottle and cooing when Chantelle Holiday, the diva—'Susanna' in the Mozart opera—returned, inspired but exhausted from having given her all, gold braids and white dress hanging rather loose.

"We would love to have seen your show," Margaret said, still beaming and visibly overcome with gratitude and awe at being given her daughter back. "If circumstances had allowed..."

Old Antioch, who had no more fashionable attire than the white shirt, brown vest, string tie and suspenders that were in fact his uniform, was equally awe-struck by the concern and warmth of this remarkable birdlike little woman. "Could you at least favor us with one of the songs?" he said, surprising even himself by asking.

Spontaneously, almost literally at the drop of the *peddler's* hat, she broke into the trills of one of the show's canticles and reached out toward this transfixed admirer as she had to Philip (Giovanni) in the actual performance. And even the infant seemed to chuckle in appreciation, as the other boarders drew into the doorway to catch a look.

The golden Mme. Holiday concluded what amounted to, even there in the boarding house (maybe *especially* there) a dazzling rendition and curtsied grandly. Then, taking Alexander Antioch (called 'Alexander *Antelope*' one time by the sheriff's little daughter, Mary) by the hand, she whirled him around in a remarkably impressive dance move, to his considerable surprise—eliciting a mock look of disapproval from the enormously amused rustic mother.

Then, turning sober very quickly, the diva addressed the two of them and, seemingly, herself. "After tonight, I can see more clearly what you good people in this fine little city are up against, how you are beset by a town tyrant who ties this place and its lovely people in knots. And I know it's over the past glory and old fears versus an open, confident future for the good of everyone."

She turned to Margaret, who was holding the baby and absorbing every word. "Girl, I tell you, I'm not going anywhere for a couple of days, but if Martin bothers you further, in any way, here is my card, with my address. If he bothers or ever even threatens you, I can fill his grand Opera Hall with nothing but cobwebs."

Margaret Dunning smiled, knowing now her protector wouldn't forget. "Uh-huh," she spoke, easily giving those syllables more meaning than they'd ever had before.

PART III ➢ SUMMER

14

A REIGN OF TERROR

The mysteriously motivated healer, Iris, came wreathed in camouflaging twice more late at night in the next week, and her almost luminous being carried into old Chessler's dream life.

How could he repay such kindnesses to him? He thought to recompense her lavishly at one point by wrapping a present of a gold brick to send off with her. But to give such as a gift as that, he reflected, would be to disclose that he was not really destitute, something he dare not reveal. Because, the question would become, just how would the likes of such an old rough cob come by a gold brick? And when she tried to exchange it to somewhere, it would become, how would the likes of Iris come by one? And, from there, the spotlight would shine right back on Chessler, and there would be no escaping it! He had no bank account accessible by himself, and so had at present to make do with stashing away the bulk of his considerable wealth to await some vague conversion in the future.

Another issue for him was whether this woman was, in fact, all that she seemed—a compassionate angel of healing only desiring to give him help. Could she be, after all, an *informer* for her unspeakable relative, Martin? Not much affinity there, it *seemed*. But, still...There was no way he could know for sure.

On the following Saturday, Chessler and Daniel were out at their camp at the flowing spring, and he went down and prized out a couple of gold bricks in the absence, as usual, of travelers or visitors on the road. Until a rain squall blew up. Then, securing the same in the cache beneath the floorboards of the moldering shack alongside the old cabin, they headed back up the now-muddy wagon track toward home.

They were less than a mile from that destination when they spied the now-familiar black carriage—in daylight for the first time—closing in on their hovel and spurred the horses to arrive in time to receive old Chessler's angel of mercy there.

He guessed, and was proven right, that she had taken advantage of the rainstorm to provide a bit of cover for a daytime visit. Under her care, the infection in the wound had dwindled and gradually vanished, presaging the long task of conjuring actual healing from a circulatory system no longer quite up to the task on its own. Chessler found her bravery a source of wonder; though the certainty that a friendship had formed still remained a stretch.

◄►

Martin's days of recruitment outside the Weston County Court House on East Main for the Wyoming Volunteer Regiment he had so strongly willed into being, with the apparent backing of the state's lone congressman, Frank Mondell, had yielded far less than the results desired—a mere twenty-seven solid recruits to date. Still, Martin and associates, generally well-lubricated, rode up and down the streets, haranguing one and all to come forth and join them. Martin was unrelenting in his insistence that the octogenarian Red Cloud was scheming to amalgamate anew the tribes of the Plains and sweep in to most unmercifully wreak revenge and drive the whites out of their houses in order to reclaim the old, vast realm of savagery, treachery, and bloody insolence.

For, it was argued, what else could the periodic illegal "hunting" forays by the young of the Lakota nation and their scouts be about, if not missions of reconnaissance and training for a long-deferred day of vengeance?

And Martin should know, having observed and opposed the wily, coiled snake long since known as Chief Red Cloud since both of them were young. And, as if such were not enough of a commendation by itself, he was also (he fancied himself) the premier lifelong expert on the northern Plains on how the savage mind worked, in sum through hatred of the whites and their freedom and their way of life. He had become, in fact, the greatest living expert and judge of all of that—because he had never for a moment forgotten or denied the enemy's ways or their evil intent. And he assuredly did not intend for the naïve and the innocent of his own town and region to now fall victim through foolish neglect.

Chessler's sometime friend, Leonardo Cass, owner of a glassware shop halfway up Main Street, and one of the few of the town's denizens who might be said to not be oppressed in any obvious way by the town's tyrant, at least in Chessler's view, told him one day in mid-June about having attended a closed meeting of the city council on unrelated business, and encountering first-hand the pro-Volunteer Regiment faction's latest scheme. The mayor, it seemed, had been leaned upon at the meeting to suggest a requirement virtually guaranteeing that all able-bodied family heads would have to join and train with the Regiment.

According to what Leonardo had learned at the meeting, any who declined to register and participate would, under the new provision, be subject to a $200 fine (when a day's wages usually amounted to about 50 cents) if caught committing any chargeable infraction on the books. Even jaywalking and spitting would trigger the fine—*unless* the miscreant had already enrolled as a Regiment volunteer. The result, after a few minor infractions had resulted in such an egregious fine being levied, was expected to be a pleasing increase in volunteering, bringing out scores and even hundreds more to plan and carry out preemptive strikes on the encamped Indians come fall and, in the meantime, secure the town against surprise attack.

Leonardo, it was mentioned, had boldly voiced dissent; and only later did he realize that he'd spoken rashly.

"It strikes me the whole idea is a crock," he reported he'd said at the meeting. "Those boys from the Res, all they want to do when they come in is let off a little bit of steam. They don't intend nobody harm no how. (Though they have reason enough for grievance, Lord knows!)"

"And you're goin' to get us all killid, too, Mista Cass," the locksmith Bailey's tottering old father, Fennimore, countered him. "Why, these salvages will be a-comin' for *you* first, I guess, you old fool, for bein' such a trustin' old dolt!"

"I don't think so," Leonardo answered firmly, just beginning to feel the cold wrath of the stares of a number of those present around the table. "And don't *you* be callin' me no old goat!"

Clearly out of line, the glass salesman Leonardo hesitated, but did continue, according to his own report: "Do any of you buzzards know just how old your Chief Red Cloud is by now? I'd say that your memories are about as long and pretty as his and your teeth."

Their answers now became only stares, and the business moved directly to passage.

◄►

The next night, Chessler and his son were again graced by a late visit and treatment from Iris, arriving in black in her black-draped conveyance. She no more than had left, certainly it hadn't been even ten minutes, before a heavy knocking came at the door in the all-but pitch-black silence. Chessler warily pushed back the thick and recalcitrant door in the last flickering of the low fire, to find standing there Bailey, the heavy-set jeweler himself, whom he recognized at once, and a bigger man of similar demeanor, whom he didn't recognize.

"You're going to have to come with us and sign papers to join the Regiment, Chessler," Bailey announced. "Or else, come up wif the $200 required on the spot right now." The rough, intelligent technician spoke with the assurance of certainty that this stubborn old cretin would have neither the means to pay, nor the stamina to render satisfactory service, and so would suffer intensely the hardship he deserved.

"On what account be you chargin' me?" Chessler countered.

"Why, with clandestine, or hidden, business—on suspicion of receiving illicit goods, or besmirching the reputation of a proper personage," Bailey replied. "We saw the likely merchant stranger that plies our streets by night and trailed the vehicle to your door. And we now know who the unknown figure is. And it won't go well for you or them, I can tell you that!"

Chessler knew he dared not try to explain things. "Then, if you know the way of it, why is it you're here to nab me and not the agent?" he asked—immediately wishing he hadn't, and feeling a need to protect the lady's secret, more than his own. But, he still wasn't convinced that Bailey knew who the person was.

"Because, that one agent or merchant might could lead us to accomplices or principals," the man spoke with less certainty now.

At this, Chessler, blinded by his growing indignation, boldly excused himself and slipped into his adjoining sleeping room, coming out immediately with the money to settle the fine, which he slapped into his surprised antagonist's hand.

The latter sucked in his breath at receiving unexpectedly such a sum, amounting to nearly a year's common wages, and asked if Chessler would care to also freely confess to him the identity of his night visitor and the nature of the alleged transaction.

"To the sheriff, perhaps," Chessler offered, not unreasonably, recovering his head. And the ominous pair, thankfully, turned and left again without a word, but with his money.

◄►

Summer had arrived unobtrusively, bringing the dreaded annual separation of Daniel from his one true same-age friend, Penny. If the black-clad stranger populated Chessler's dreams, her golden-haired niece's absence left a longing just as tender in his son Daniel's heart. The two, father and son, made both a merry and a pathetic pair in those long early-summer days, riding with Red up between them on their dutiful rounds to scrub the interiors and clear the weeds from the yards of various churches of the town, making all-day forays to man their water post on the all-but-abandoned old stage road whenever they were free and their contract work done.

And, with the lengthening days, how they missed stopping by to talk with their old bosom friends, John and Luella, on the way over to their water post! And how forlorn were the house and outbuildings of their friends' little ranch place now as they passed, the yard and grounds all grown to weeds, all the valuables left having been picked clean by "strangers" within two days after the crime was announced. Chessler privately suspected that these "strangers" were the same ones who had abducted and strung up the purported killer a few weeks later to enforce what he could only see as a very peculiar and insincere brand of "justice." And maybe, too, they were the same as those model citizens hiding behind string ties and bowler hats at the hushed-up council meeting Leonardo Cass had told him about. At least some of them probably had been there.

Now, as they passed the Churches' ranch, slowing in reverence and curiosity, the chicken yard was strangely silent and still, and in Luella's flower garden, the high heads of last year's hollyhocks still swayed in the wind, listening patiently for their benefactors' delayed return. Their cat Bubi, gone feral now, was glimpsed dashing between the clap-trap fallen-down structures. The crick still ran clear with a gurgling noise over the rocks beside the road. They saw John's horseshoe collection still nailed to the fence, with only one or two of the unusual ones missing. It wasn't safe, they told themselves, to linger there for long.

The problem was: How to keep on getting Iris's healing, so vital for the recovery of his leg, without further endangering the angel-nurse herself? When she came the next time, they warned her that the powers-that-be of the town were onto her night visits and had already exacted tribute. They might not yet know, from mere reports, just who was traveling the streets and paths in the night, so shadowy and elusive a figure had she been. But, they surely would know soon.

At least for now, she allowed, it would be wise to instruct Daniel in applying the medical materials and see he was provided therewith. It was not the ideal course to follow, perhaps, but she knew he was a good learner. Having shown him how to administer the medicines and dressings as best she could, she gently shook her patient's hand with her small one and silently kissed Daniel on the cheek. And then she was gone, arrangements made for periodic pick-ups of supplies on future days.

So far, with its inestimable presidential visit—something that some in Newcastle still filed in their brains as more dream than historical happening—and its two privileged performances by the Chicago Opera Company on successive nights, the town was, by the middle of 1903, riding the crest of an enormous tide of pride and self-congratulation, Diamond L. Clifton be damned. At least until three weeks later, when a news wire bulletin arrived informing that Chantelle Holiday, the famous diva, had collapsed on board the train and was diagnosed with arsenic poisoning after leaving on the weekend prior. She had only been saved by the heroic ministration, involving infusion of carbon, by a Dr. Keller at the renowned opera company's next stop, Scottsbluff. Margaret Dunning, when she heard of it, began to clutch her precious little Judy Anne more tightly than ever, and prayed with a fervor beyond any known in the town.

But, in fact, Sheriff Miller wasn't specially apprised to seek the poisoners; and, interestingly, the news of it barely reached the first pages of the *News-Journal*. Instead, their lead article had to do with plans for a gigantic Fourth of July celebration and parade, featuring the Wyoming Volunteer Regiment, now almost five-hundred strong, marching in uniform, these to be followed by a contingent of nineteen soldiers from Fort Fred Steele in the southern part of the state. Fort Steele, it was noted as a sidelight, was just about the only currently-active military post left, Fort Laramie having closed fifteen years ago, and Fetterman before that.

Come the Fourth, Chessler and Daniel stood along the parade route at the foot of the hill on mid-Main Street. Chessler had heard via Cass of the rude protest by part of individuals in the Opera Hall audience, and expected to hear at least some talk about that, or indignant mention of the departed Slim or the Churches on the Fourth.

But he personally heard no such talk. Instead, all in attendance on a perfect summer day, a little hot but with a breeze, were in a festive mood, each attendee as finely dressed as his or her circumstances would allow. Even, or perhaps especially, the foreign-born coal-miners he knew, from east end Newcastle and Cambria, were in a carefree patriotic uniquely Fourth of July mood.

The two from outside the town spotted Penny, with Iris, some ways away, exchanged waves and smiles, but felt unfree to go over and talk with them.

The parade was actually led, it turned out, by the visiting fife and drum corps from Fort Steele, playing martial and patriotic songs, followed closely by other soldiers in dress blue, marching in formation, and a few on horseback. These were followed by the throng of active paramilitary Volunteer Regiment members, mostly middle-aged and older, led by Bailey and Martin on horses. Manfred rode a little behind, followed by others, some in cavalry colors and a lot in faded and sagging uniforms from wars of the past generation, including Union Army uniforms, and some in ordinary clothes. Two even dared don their gray uniforms of the

Confederacy. Younger and older soldiers of the various wars straggled still farther back, lacking discernible organization. Behind these came a women's Nursing Corps unit, dressed smartly, but only about a dozen in number, marching shoulder to shoulder in a single line. And so it eventuated that the preponderance of observers lining the street that day were females.

The thought crossed Chessler's mind, as it always did on these occasions, how absurd and futile it was for both sides in any clash of arms to send out both the gunners to annihilate and medical units to try and patch up those who got shot up, on whichever side, and in most cases carrying on fights that were themselves entirely unnecessary and tragic. As if to punctuate this private, preposterous point, perhaps clear in his mind alone, an ancient artillery piece commandeered by the Wyoming Volunteer Regiment fired off twice at intervals live shells that sailed away above the buildings and landed no doubt with a clatter or clunk on empty streets beyond. Ironically enough for him, the old field piece resembled mightily (and may actually have *been*) the very cannon Chessler himself had incapacitated clandestinely in the first incarnation of the Wyoming Volunteers, decades before.

At the very end of the parade, came the rodeo clowns driving and riding in an old stagecoach and (rationally or not), last of all, a certain Dr. Morris up from Lusk, the first real town to the south—the former home of Deputy Johnny Owens—driving his truly amazing horseless carriage, a cunning little monstrosity he had ordered from an Eastern newspaper, and the first such known in that part of Wyoming. He was joined in his "car" for part of the route by Mr. Mondell, the Congressman, still hanging out and hobnobbing around Newcastle.

When the procession came to a halt on the level area of street at the top of the hill, onlookers not surprisingly surrounded the tall, dignified-looking elderly doctor from the neighboring town, to touch and visually inspect his curious—if loud and smoky—vehicle and ask a hundred questions, to which Dr. Morris seemed to have all the answers.

Meanwhile, Sheriff Miller, along with Deputy Owens and Joe LeFors, were sighted standing on the edge of the street at approximately the halfway point of the route. Their significant others and, in Miller's case, his gang of children, were not immediately conspicuous beside them, but might have been found farther below, near the cotton candy man.

Banners held aloft by the biggest contingent of marchers read: "Nits Make Lice" and "Your Wyoming Volunteer Regiment Protects Property and Home."

The rustic pair who were consigned to the last dugout for a home could not help but overhear the young Fort Steele soldiers afterward mocking and arguing loudly with the "platoon leaders" of the Volunteer Regiment who helped raise the giant signs. These present-day soldiers vociferously championed the need in modern times for an emphasis on peace and harmony instead of war in the West and baldly asserted the baselessness going into the twentieth century of fears and presumably provocations involving the defeated aboriginal natives.

The youngsters of both sexes lining the route, though, seemed duly dazzled by all the smart and even essentially makeshift soldiery passing by. The only Indian to be seen that day was a masked mock-up on a swayback horse being jostled by the rodeo clown, with a big gun firing smoky and reverberating blanks and the mounted clown's wicked-looking sword terrifying the foe.

All in all, all were suitably entertained and awed by the somewhat expanded annual spectacle.

◀▶

On the reservation at Pine Ridge, the Fourth of July celebration organized by Superintendent John Brennan was more subdued, with riders on war ponies whooping it up a bit out on the parade ground with three Lakota veterans of the Battle of San Juan Hill in army uniform. One man rode three bulls successively in a demonstration and the kids from Pine Ridge played a team from Valentine in baseball, losing 23 to 2 in seven innings.

That night in his lodge, with his squaw Little Fawn lying by his side, Eagle Feather had a recurrent dream. He was back at Carlisle School, where football had become a serious game by '96, at which the Indians—mostly giving up something in terms of bulk—had learned they could beat the big white schools only through effective use of superior smarts, determination, and deception.

They played the toughest of the white teams that year, Yale, on a field in Manhattan, and as the end of the game neared, the lightly regarded Indian team had managed to pull within a single touchdown, at 12 to 6. Charlie Smith (Eagle Feather), a reserve, remembered it as clearly as if it been that afternoon. The Indians' frenzied rooters, which by that time included nearly everyone present, since they were putting up such a scrap, urgently reminded them that time was running out, and they had to score on their current possession to preserve a tie. And they did, with a long touchdown run on a deceptive crisscross play, in which the man the Yale players thought had the ball didn't. Jamison, who had the ball, had fooled all but two of the Yalies. They caught him briefly at the 35-yard line, but he broke free and scored.

Still, the referee's whistle had blown when he was caught, and accordingly, the referee's mistake, not the action on the field, was what was honored and counted, and the game was given to Yale over bitter Carlisle protests. And in Charlie Smith's dream, their complaints sounded like super-loud kazoos that continued to buzz on and on and on.

Just as with Little Big Horn and Red Cloud's effective closing of the Bozeman Road before that, Eagle Feather thought—the white man wins out in what counts, the final score, even as he loses to the Indians in the contest! And, not only that, but the powerful and sufficient means the Indians had of maintaining their independent strength and insuring survival, the bison and the health of the vast range, were destroyed. And the Indians of the Plains, as had been the case with Indians everywhere else earlier, had been confined and reduced in cramped outdoor prisons where they were expected to eventually die as distinct peoples, and then as individuals. That was the stuff of Eagle Feather's worst nightmare, sometimes with lions or bears, sometimes with masks on the players, sometimes, more ominously, played with ghosts and bison skulls.

The game itself, Charlie Smith/Eagle Feather only reminded himself of what he knew, had been introduced at Carlisle to teach that very lesson. The Indians might be better, but they were never allowed to win in real life. And even his assigned legal name, Charlie Smith, removed an Indian!

His woman, Little Fawn, as always, surrendered to his endlessly flailing arms and got up to boil tea.

15

PLENTY COUP, SUFFERED AND COUNTED

Eagle Feather pondered many things that summer. He watched his own little daughter and younger son as they scooted in and out of his canvas lodge, yelling and arms and legs churning, not an care apparent in the world. And what was their destiny in this world? They didn't know it yet—no one had explained it to them, and it was certainly none of their doing—that they had been born into a prison population, dependent utterly on the "Great White Father" for everything, while they themselves now had nothing, no waiting legacy, since the great kill-off of the buffalo and the denial of freedom of access to the land where buffalo had so recently swarmed that there was still plentiful sign of them.

As for Eagle Feather himself, one of his earliest childhood memories was of the victorious chiefs leading the powerful and beautiful braves back from their great victory over Custer—"Yellow Hair." But then there followed the unending buffalo slaughter by the whites with the heavy rifles, defeats mounting where there had been victories. And the worm had turned. Sitting Bull retreated to Canada and Crazy Horse, suddenly with neither guns nor horses to sustain him, was forced to surrender, and grew taciturn and sullen, before being treacherously killed in captivity.

Chief Red Cloud, the man who had effectively shut down the road to Montana gold camps that was splitting his people's lands, was more realistic, it appeared to many. He looked to his people's welfare instead of pursuing abstract principles where there was no means and the need was growing more severe by the day. He got Crazy Horse to surrender and guaranteed his cooperation, and now, here they were.

Eagle Feather/Charlie Smith had a somewhat quiet friend from a family of prominent warriors named Amos Bad Heart Bull, who recorded the stories of past deeds against the whites and Crows in particular, as told him by his uncles, in skillful paintings in a ledger book. Amos Bad Heart Bull told Eagle Feather that the solution to the Lakota's plight lay in the attitude of refusing to acknowledge defeat. If the Oglala Lakota could stand fast in spite of their present adversity, they would survive until things got better. They must refuse to weaken and not falter, believing that help would come. Bad Heart Bull's words, which he said he learned from communing with Red Cloud, made an impression. Smith/Feather believed that ultimately the Lakota must make their own luck; but he acknowledged there weren't always the means at hand.

And, though it offered no way out of the present difficulties, what may have been missing from Eagle Feather's tragic understanding of realities was that only a hundred years before the whites began to arrive in numbers, the Sioux people of the buffalo-rich Plains arrived from the east and pushed the long-time occupant tribes back into the mountains and conditions of terrible hunger and misery, just as the whites expanding across the land had lately dispossessed the Sioux. And to cry when what goes comes back to you is not even Lakota. And so, who would in time oppress the whites?

◄►

Martin knew that the situation regarding the protection of the county and town was getting desperate. He'd have to whip all these raw new recruits into shape. As things stood, their bumbling around wouldn't even slow the invaders.

He'd often talked about it with Bailey, whom he was convinced was the only one who truly understood his best thinking, and together they had come up with two different theories as to how Red Cloud's invaders (or "Cloud-Head's" as they sometimes referred to that infernal salvage) might try to advance.

They might try to do so directly, by knocking off a few outlying ranch places—unprotected sitting ducks—in order to gain possible fortifiable sites for themselves to attack from, and to lure contingents of the Regiment of Volunteers out into the open and pick them off. Hoping to frighten the weak-hearted in the town (or towns, if Cambria and Upton be included) to flee their homes in the West and go back to where they came from, leaving the towns more vulnerable.

Or, they might try to sabotage the rail and road lines into Newcastle, just as Red Cloud had earlier attacked and shut down the Bozeman Road access to Montana.

Either way, their objective would be to get the whites to ease their civilized grip on the land the Sioux and their friends had once made uninhabitable except for some very hardy whites who knew how to take care of themselves in a raw and savage land.

Red Cloud, Martin knew for sure, knew how to make a few friends count as many in strategic effectiveness. Had the Indians no horses and no rifles, as their apologists suggested? True, they didn't have many. But by the simple act of knocking over a few ranches, one by one, they would be able to gain both.

And so, to defeat their plan, Martin was eager to tell all who would listen, his voice now like a raw wind blowing out between his tight-set jaws, past the snaggle gaps between his few teeth. And he planned to mercilessly drill all who would stand up to add to the protection. And then, he would lead them out onto the prairie to slaughter the advancing braves, engaged in their true and serious business camouflaged by the ruse of a hunt.

And those in the town who wouldn't enlist even to protect themselves must at least be made to pay the expenses of their protectors; and, perhaps (unannounced) to move into the front ranks, to at least insulate the braver men and women of the town from rapid attack.

Which brought him to the point—what about the *women*? He reckoned they could at least be requisitioned and conscripted into service to the men. Which was their role, anyway, when he thought about it.

Martin planned a series of rallies, with bonfires and bands and speakers, to raise the martial spirit of the lackadaisical town. And he announced it and his "Council of the Valiant" all drank to the idea and drank another round in honor of him and his efforts.

◄►

On August 3, 1903, the leading ladies of Newcastle kept alive a tradition started four years earlier on the thirtieth anniversary (as accounted, or fancied, by some) of the tea party a stout pioneer woman, Esther Morris, was supposed to have held out in the raw gold mining camp of South Pass City, in Wyoming Territory, at the time in only its first year of existence. The significance of that storied tea party, to honor a pair of legislative candidates, was that it marked the effective birth of the notion—which took hold there first—of codifying into law the political equality of women and men.

And so, the ladies of Weston County inaugurated a dance on that largely arbitrary date, to which they took the lead by inviting each of them a man. And after three years of "too busy," "can't dance," and other excuses, Anna Miller had finally gotten her Billy to accompany her and together, put their best foot forward.

Billy thought it a little silly, since there were train robberies going on, aggravated murders, and horse rustlings in distant and not-so-distant parts of the state to potentially solve with LeFors and other colleagues. And since, according to him, a man with two left feet couldn't be expected to cut much of a figure and ought not to embarrass his wife. But she wouldn't hear of any of it this particular year, and with just a little patient instruction and an application of loving persuasion, he proved himself wrong and a natural as a dancer—at least, with her.

A six-piece orchestra of local musicians played, and some of the songs were decidedly upbeat and were said to have come from a music-writer in Kansas City whose name was Joppa or Java, or something like that. The night was definitely something different and something memorable.

Whether the date of the anniversary or the authenticity of the occasion was right or not was beyond the knowing of anybody local. But it made for a popular occasion, and did commemorate something very special that all women of Wyoming were justly proud of, and even some of the men. The temperance ladies had gotten control of it this year, agreement to alternate years, and so nothing stronger than a little cider was served. But none seemed to need livening anyway, the music and the company being ample. And, as for Billy, he lightened and sweetened, just as Anna had hoped.

Johnny Owens looked in at one point, even though the ball was held in the city hall and not his establishment. He complimented the music, and it was clear to at least some of the women that he surely felt subdued and hamstrung—and not just for the occasion. In sober fact, the third wife he had for so long nursed and, frankly, put up with as not overly supportive of him, was a semi-invalid now and not of a disposition to any longer enjoy the sort of fun times they had once shared. But faithful he was, almost for sure.

◄►

A day or two later, Chessler was amazed to read in the latest number of the *News-Tribune* that Indians had been caught raiding area ranches, stealing chickens and, in one instance, rustling cattle and/or horses. They were glimpsed lurking around the edges, seen on the old stage road and other connecting routes singly and in pairs, presumably scouting out places to take over and fortify for their planned armed forays against the towns. This story, lacking details and giving the names of only one or two ranch owners, whom Chessler had never heard of, was found, strangely, only in a special supplement, but splashed all over a couple of pages in bold print. And Chessler, whose upfront business was on what would no doubt be the leading road, never heard or saw sign of any such activity, extremely unlikely in itself in that day—except in the paper.

But lots of residents were shocked and upset by the revelations, and within days, Martin had the Antlers Hotel special defenses completed and called for new, intense drills of the Wyoming Volunteer Regiment that Saturday at the school athletic field. By night, even in a light rain, he once more rode the streets on his big old gray horse, accompanied by others of the "Loungers," yelling essentially, "See, it's just as I've been telling you! Those who love their families and their town and the white man's civilization in this part of the country, come out with your rifles and join us! Drill and expedition this Saturday morning at dawn, and no Indians will be allowed to live in this section of Wyoming! And no friends of the Indian...You're either with us, or you're with the savages!"

The tyrant Martin got wind that Victor Grant Smith, perhaps the greatest buffalo slayer of all time—mostly in the 1880s—was coming in from his Idaho home to visit his niece, and would be arriving in Newcastle that Friday. After contacting the famous hunter, he organized a banquet in his honor at the hotel for that evening and strongly urged his entire volunteer unit and the townspeople to attend.

At the huge banquet, possibly the largest mass feast in the history of Newcastle, organized and served by the city's church women, Martin introduced the guest of honor, a completely ordinary-looking man, to whom he suggested he had long and close ties, as "perhaps the greatest Wyoming Indian fighter of all time," though he had never drawn a bead on a red man. No, he just removed their food supply and opened up the Plains to civilized white man's cattle.

And then, old Vic, from the lectern, told a story Martin couldn't have paid him to concoct, putting the already legendary Sioux in a new light from what anyone had ever seen them in.

Old "Yellowstone Vic" told of the time in his travels when he had stumbled onto a Lakota encampment, and the Indians were found in the act of roasting a large dog over a fire—luscious fare for them. Vic, their guest, was reading a book by the firelight over at one side, when the Sioux bade him to come and partake of the dog feast. Realizing that he had better comply, and seeing all the Indians' rifles at the ready, and at full cock, he put a little of the meat in his mouth.

At this, the Indians, he said, were circling around him and pointing their rifles and yelling very loudly. So, he knew he'd better keep eating. He gorged himself on dog meat for three hours, and then they insisted that, stuffed and showing signs of being just a bit queasy, he run the gauntlet for their entertainment.

Then, at least in his telling (impossible to verify, but not doubted), he was stripped naked ("stripped *noo-ood*", he emphasized, and all the kids snickered), and forced to shoot bullets, champion shot that he was, so as to outline a condemned adulteress's entire naked body closer than an inch without killing her, then ordered to draw blood, which he did minimally. Then, both of them were released to wend their way unclothed and at top speed to a somewhat distant fort.

Old Vic warned the audience of hundreds sweltering in the gas-lit banquet hall to forget their illusions about Indian civility and take precaution. And the audience ate it up.

Incredibly, the very next morning, word started to spread quietly and slowly through the town that, on Jasper Jones's ranch, six miles out, a "tall Indian with a lone feather" had been spotted raiding a chicken coop and chased off by the owner's near neighbor, Roy Jeffrey, only to find a Pine Ridge Reservation Enrollment Card with the name of Big Ears, next to an Esther Morris dance invitation with Martin's son Manfred's name engraved on it, on the ground just outside the open door to the coop. Later, rancher Jones, who was not supposed to have been there originally, swore to another neighbor, Robert Edwards, according to the story being told, that that was "one Indian who wouldn't be able to sit down for a year" due to a good full load of buckshot.

16

QUEASY

The golden days of Daniel's summer were passing like the fleecy clouds over-head, and very soon, pellets of snow would be wafting and shooting horizontally again above the frozen prairie. July had turned into August and, as that month wore on, the mellow warmth of the days began to be replaced by a hint of a tang in the early morning, and locusts were on the wing. Daniel had landed a job of his own—a sort of job—as assistant and back-up delivery boy for the weekly *Newcastle News-Journal* for the western half of the town, because he owned one of only two functioning bicycles among boys without superior means or steady employment. And, occasionally, he substituted for the regular carrier on the east side, during his asthma attacks.

In the latter sort of instance, he was over by the school on August 16, and watched the strictly civilian recruits of the Wyoming Volunteer Regiment in their drills on the school athletic grounds. He observed their rifle range and concluded two things: First, not taking the alleged Indian menace seriously, he hoped these old codgers would relinquish the playing field back to the boys in time for their ball practice, and, second, he knew it would be futile to put these duffers in charge of defending the town in case it ever were attacked.

Chessler and Daniel had, weeks before, received a letter mailed by Iris with instructions for their wound care, and to pick up supplies for same, to be secreted in the culvert beneath a particular street where it crossed a small stream that was a known landmark. And a parcel wrapped in foil was always there waiting on the day appointed.

The wound seemed to be responding slowly to the treatment of silver nitrate solution, and the antibiosis tablets Iris supplied eliminated the infection that had threatened to take old Chessler's lower leg, or something more serious. Still, the patient mourned the loss of the kind nurse's evaluation and experience.

In the meantime, the two of them managed to locate and secretly recover, and cache under the rotting floor, at least two more gold bricks, or bars, each week. And Chessler continued to ponder it all.

A mystery to him was the private attitude of the respective Sheriff Miller and his ever more frequent collaborator Owens toward the anti-Indian civilian force and measures. Even close up, he observed, the reaction from that quarter seemed ambivalent.

The demeanor of most of the town, though, was apparently becoming more fearful and willing to adopt extreme and violent measures to counter savagery of the sort now continually reported or rumored to be taking place daily not far distant in the surrounding prairies, and each time closer to the town. Since the birth of Newcastle, with the exception of a year or two when outlaws had seriously threatened public order, this was, in fact, the first time public security had been in doubt.

Early on Monday morning of the week after the first disturbing reports had come in, the Deputy had broached his own doubts of the reports' authenticity to the sheriff. Entering Sheriff Miller's office, where the serving peace officer sat hunkered at his desk, noticeably tense, Johnny Owens approached him and suggested he take a breather.

"But how can I relax," Sheriff Miller responded, "when half the county is risen in arms to resume hostilities against any poor Indian that might appear? And one or more does occasionally, you know. The strongest defense forces in the area now are not now under the command, or even influence, of the duly-constituted authorities. And we must be ever mindful of that."

"Well, you could order them to stand down," Johnny suggested. "You know there's nothing to the stories."

"Oh, really? You were aware that Sioux Indians have been arrested and jailed right behind you in the recent past for hunting illegally in this jurisdiction? They do show up, you know. And people do hear about it, and are, naturally, fearful."

"But you handled it! And it didn't take half the town to control it. Nor would it again."

"But you—of all people—know the politics of this place, Owens."

"Yeah. And I'd buck it again, too," Johnny Owens said, and walked briskly out. Then, sticking his head back in and looking the present sheriff in the eye, he added: "Bill, you know that Red Cloud has nothing to do with it."

◄►

Oddly, it seemed to the public at large that Martin's inebriation and aloofness—casting him almost in a man-on-horseback role—actually contributed to his credibility and growing attraction, as an earnest if handicapped leader. He was observed as one who sacrificed to lead and led in spite of the difficulty and superficial implausibility, of it. Someone who may fall off his horse and slur his words at times, but whose determined heart and keen will gave him a credible and consistent call, one who would save the town he had practically built to provide so very many with a good and comfortable home they now needed to help him protect. The churches recruited and collected for the Regiment from the pulpit, casting the Indians as fearsome devils and Red Cloud as at least an evil shade or precursor of the Antichrist. The stories of the old bygone days of the Great Sioux War, as told by the precious few who remembered, were dragged out and reveled in again. Certainly, the participation of a good citizen seemed a small price to pay for all that they all had.

So, in the process of preparing a credible defense, the hotel and Court House were additionally fortified, walls were erected, and trenches and latrines dug strategically along the back streets. Now, the few lone riders, led by Martin, who had at first looked like such buffoons, were replaced by platoons of marching men led by a quartermaster and smartly, in formation, saluting the Stars & Stripes and the Great State of Wyoming buffalo flag. And rations and armaments were stacked in a city armory, with stalls to tether two hundred horses. By the end of August, this defense thing was decidedly real.

There was talk of postponing the start of school, to avoid children being stranded alone in the streets, or in the open in the event of an attack, or of the hilltop school being surrounded.

In the midst of the combination autocratic order and frantic turmoil, Iris traveled again at night on September 1 in her black bunting-camouflaged carriage, up to check and confer with Chessler and his boy. It became apparent that she was unwilling to abandon her patient, even under dire circumstances, and she made it apparent that she, too, put no stock whatsoever in the cry of danger or the "leaders" who had declared it.

Chessler, disappearing without a word for a moment back through the curtain into his dark sleeping chamber, returned with a sizeable chunk knocked off one of the encrusted gold bars, which he slipped unnoticed into his benefactor's black bag, as sleight of hand while serving her a piece of cake from the bakery along the middle of Main Street. He imagined that she could at least bank that amount without drawing undue suspicion; and that amount would also not seem so incredible to her that he might have come by it honorably in some way.

And then, after satisfying herself that his leg was improving, she slipped away again as silently as she had come.

◂▸

Shortly after midnight on that night, Tuesday, September 1, the main city water tank was blown up, with a resounding dull *crack* heard throughout the town, and the precious fluid surged down Birch Street in a wave, floating dogs off porches and filling basements. People ran out of their houses in response to the noise and stood in the cool air in their nightclothes and shawls, murmuring and commiserating and shouting to neighbors about what on earth could have occurred.

A drunk weaving toward home on foot, and then others after him, declared that four or five ghostly Indian figures had been seen to ride eastward immediately afterward out of town. Before long, Martin came riding along, whipping his horse into a gallop, then reigning up successively to two or three places to address the people as to what they had heard or witnessed. He blamed it on the Sioux and declared that the Volunteer Regiment would ride out to avenge the act early the next day. Intended or not, his declaration seemed to supersede the call of the mayor—made just before—for volunteers to work on an emergency crew reporting the next morning to repair or rebuild the wooden structure and, in the meantime, deliver emergency water rations to all affected homes.

The next morning, Deputy Sheriff Owens, who had overnighted out on his ranch, returned home and encountered firsthand accounts of the giant water tank explosion while stopping in for breakfast at Arthur's Roadhouse on the northeast edge of town. An acquaintance named Fred Davies, who was a sheep auctioneer, came over to his table to tell him, and when he came to the part about the four or five Sioux Indians having done it, Owens stopped him cold.

"How do you mean?" he asked.

"Well, everybody knows they've been lurking around, and—"

"Really? Didn't you hear about Martin's son Manfred's dance card turning up on the ground out at Jasper Jones's ranch, where the chicken house was broken into?"

"Well, yes, but also...I don't know. Martin said that didn't mean anything, and..."

"Martin said, Martin said. I haven't seen any Indians around here, have you?"

"Well, no, but..."

"You say they was seen moving east...by a drunk? Did anybody try to catch up with them?"

"No. Sheriff said..."

By that time, John Owens had swallowed his pancake and paid his bill and was halfway to ask the Sheriff himself.

"Bill," he said minutes later, walking quietly up behind Miller writing at his desk.

Sheriff Miller, startled, turned around, and Johnny continued. "Did you go and try to catch up with those supposed Indians who were headed out toward the east last night?"

"No," answered Billy Miller politely. "It was just a drunk coming home from a bar who said he'd seen them."

"But Martin showed up immediately, then, and made something big out of it? Like proof that the Indians he said were coming, to wipe out the town, were already making an appearance?"

"Yeah, that's what he said," Sheriff Miller agreed. "Not what I said."

"Well, do you believe it? Because I think I know what's going on."

"Well, you know, they were around the area last year. And they will be back!"

"Not like that, though."

"Look. I can't stop him. I can't even talk to him about it if I want to."

"If you want to? Well, maybe not. But, there comes a time, and—"

"I know, John, I know."

Owens left the office steaming and shaking his head. But he really couldn't get up his ire at Sheriff Billy Miller, the one man he never came to figure out, to know whether to admire or pity.

But still, he had to try and reason with people, so he made a tour of downtown, talking with everyone he ran into.

"Well, I'm headed for the defense drill up at the athletic field now," many of the men he encountered told him.

"But you don't believe the Sioux Lakota are a threat to attack the town, and that some have already been brazenly raiding and attacking, do you?"

"Yes. They was here and did that last night. I practically seen them. And one man did. Them Sioux mean business!"

"But how do you know who they were, who did it?"

"Well, given the choice between Injuns done it and who knows who, I'm pickin' the Injuns. That's what old Martin says happened. And old Martin, he knows."

Johnny just stared in people's faces, stupefied and dismayed that they could be so duped and blind.

"We're gonna get on our horses in a couple days and give them Injuns... leastwise, the ones that's campin' and raidin' around here, what fer!" another man said.

"But, that's the sort of thing that's...you know, a crime," Owens said, "that we gather evidence for, fingerprints and the like, and apply due process for. Due process! Have you heard of that? Arresting them and a trial and so on..."

"Why? We already know who done it! Who else would a' done it?"

Johnny supposed he'd be stating and re-stating and answering the same points, over and over and over, for at least the next several days, not wanting to make it clear just yet whom he strongly suspected had really done it and why. Because, he couldn't imagine that Weston County was ready for *that*...that is, to entertain *reasoned* doubts. Not for the moment, at least.

A few days later, now well into September, the mail coach coming through from Custer, South Dakota pulled up in front of the rickety cinderblock administration building in the little burg of Pine Ridge, South Dakota, and the driver walked into the superintendent's outer office and dumped the usual sheaf of letters, and an open copy of the current *Newcastle News-Journal,* on top of long-necked Major John R. Brennan's desk.

Rushing in from a counseling session with a family at the café on a ghastly grit-blown day, slicking his hair down by force of habit before going over budget matters with a young assistant, Superintendent Brennan glanced down and caught the headline on the unfamiliar paper: "Lakota Sioux Depredations." He looked again. This—whatever it meant, and it couldn't be right—he knew was going to compromise and make impossible the now-critical decision he was being pressured to make and carry out in the next two weeks. It was as if thirty years had fallen like autumn leaves from the calendar.

PART IV ➢ FALL

17

A SQUARE DEAL

To contend that John R. Brennan was "popular with the Oglala Lakota of Pine Ridge"—as some reports have pronounced—would be an oversimplification of the situation. It would be more true to say they liked having him in charge because they could find ways of finessing him to get their way most of the time.

Brennan, whom his charges routinely referred to as "Long Neck," waged his own perennial battles, one of which was to get the Bureau of Indian Affairs in Washington to finally construct him a comfortable office. The one he occupied, a holdover from the agency's earliest days, was excessively drafty, conducive to sand and dust, and a veritable ice box in winter. Another unending battle was to preserve the unoccupied, neutral strip across the reservation's southern boundary in northern Nebraska, in order to keep the whiskey sellers farther away and harder to reach for the vulnerable and too-often besotted Oglala.

He certainly didn't need the obviously bogus story he read about in the Newcastle paper to be circulating all over three states, weeks before he was contemplating authorizing his pressing young wards' desperately desired travel plan for a fall hunt—repeating forays of recent years—back in the old traditional hunting grounds to the west. With the handful of settlers in that area—mainly in Newcastle—on edge, inexplicably thinking that some Indians were already lurking around and conducting furtive raids, and—*incredibly*—ready to attack with full force, it would be unthinkable to send them off hunting in that direction.

But even from two hundred miles away, he could formulate in his mind what must lay behind the shockingly false published reports there on his desk. He fancied he knew, or could see through, that bigoted blowhard big-shot Martin, who ran things over there. In a sort of negative way, they went way back. And Martin, he surmised, was the source of the reports and probably of some sort of cobbled-together incidents to blame on Indians. He never had known a man so insanely anti-Indian as that clown, who had sent him dozens of ranting and infantile letters threatening him with all manner of repercussions should Sioux Indians ever again set foot in Weston County or that whole section of Wyoming.

Well, this Martin, who he personally had thrown in a river and out of town once long ago for his bigotry, didn't merit any kind of positive response or notice from him, and never got one. So now, Martin must have figured that spreading the report that Lakota Indians were present and raiding thereabouts would discourage him from permitting his young men's travels that fall, and get him what he had been demanding. And then, if he, Brennan, persisted in sending them, the Wyoming folks would be stirred up and ready to make them wish they'd stayed back in their cramped box.

"Stark raving sane, madly lucid, that one," the Irishman thought. And there were further complications to consider as well.

The old warrior, Chief Red Cloud, perhaps the most famous Indian then living in the United States, had come only a few days before to speak with him about the matter. Red Cloud said he had had a dream in which the younger warriors were on their journey and encountered buffalo near Powder River. He had surprised Brennan—*"Long Neck"*—by stating that his dream for certain had foretold the truth, and that he believed that buffalo would be sighted exactly as in his dream. Accordingly, he proposed to Brennan a wager. If proof could be produced when the party returned that buffalo had been spotted, it would be agreed that Major Brennan would recommend to Washington that self-rule be returned to the Lakota. And, if such proof could not be produced, the often-troublesome Red Cloud agreed to back up Brennan in whatever decisions he should make as long as both of them were around.

And the old chief had warned Brennan ominously when he left that, if he refused to allow the young bucks their desired hunt, it was he who would have a war on his hands. Brennan shuddered, knowing for certain that that would be the worst alternative. Let the buffoon stew!

◀▶

Old Chessler continued to get his supplies every Wednesday stashed at the appointed repository, for Daniel to carefully apply according to their angel Iris's instructions, into mid-September. And then, one week he sent Daniel to ride his bicycle to fetch the package and bring it back—*and it wasn't there.* So, they had to stretch such supplies as were remaining farther than usual. In truth, Chessler's leg wound didn't seem to be healing anymore, but just maintaining, neither getting any better nor worse. But, what to make of the breakdown in the supply system, they didn't know.

Back at school, Daniel inquired about Iris of Penny, and found out she was okay, but seemed to be tired and worried about something that, when Penny asked her about it, she always just dismissed with a sad smile and a wave of her hand.

◄►

Daniel had as good an imagination as any boy ever had. He was a bit shambling and no athlete, and for too long had been shunned to boot. But he liked to watch baseball on the school diamond, when the reds played the blues, or, occasionally, a team from Upton, Cambria, Osage, and once from Custer—a team so big and fast they left Newcastle's all-stars in the dust in the first contest, but won over them by just a little, 19 to 15, in the second. The men (mostly downtown merchants) played the team from the school once, and found out they weren't as superior or hot as they'd assumed.

Daniel read with great relish—as did several other boys—the daily reports off the telegraph wire Mr. Gammage at the *News-Journal* issued reporting the first-ever "World Series" of baseball in October of 1903, between the Pittsburgh Pirates and the Boston Americans. Daniel Edgemont, like boys all over America that year, knew the great pitcher Cy Young, Honus Wagner, Clark, Dineen, Leceh, Collins, and other participants from posters and sports news reports. Old Chessler's boy, just like many other boys, had only actually seen a diamond of dirt and local heroes as real players, but knew all about the American and National League teams and players, and imagined in their minds local fields and stands for scores of yelling fans simply being multiplied, with the noise and excitement multiplied, a thousand-, ten-thousand fold! And, in their minds, they saw every play in those final, championship games that were depicted in wire-source print. Little else mattered for a week or more, when The Game was the world!

Hot off the press by late morning of October 2 came the special sheet with the opening-day report, with Gammage, grinning like a gargoyle, passing it down the line to the boys, and a couple of men, eagerly waiting on the sidewalk in front of the news building. (Boston, Huntington Avenue Base Ball Grounds): Pittsburgh beat Cy Young's Boston Americans by 7 to 3, although Boston, favored by the more well-mannered and courteous boys and not a few girls, came back in the late innings. Meanwhile, some of the rougher sorts of boys, who naturally favored the "Pirates," went around after news of the outcome of the game, whacking the more sedate boys on the back of the head, knocking hats askew, and whooping like Indians, eliciting yells of "quit it!" all down upper Main Street.

When the next morning's edition of the fly sheet for the second game came out, on Saturday, so there was no school, the better-balanced partisans, no one knowing the score of Friday's game till then, felt they had their revenge, as they all learned how the Boston team's defensive play had secured the second contest for them, 3 to 0.

The fans in Newcastle School—and only the older ones were permitted to lope down the hill and pick up the weekday championship series dispatch—may have been as fascinated and anxious regarding the games as those on the scene. But they had to wait until Monday to learn the result of the Saturday game, the last played in Boston before the serried moved.

By now, the role of favorite had already shifted from the Pirates to the more clean-cut and well-behaved (at least in their image in Newcastle) Boston Americans. That was true, at least, until the report passed out Monday disclosed that Boston fans had shown up by the thousands, way more than the number of seats, and mounted an unseemly riot for admittance. To top it off, Pittsburgh stole the game 4 to 2, casting a gloomy pall over everyone, both inside and outside. That is, everyone except for the Pirates and their low-class partisans.

Daniel, feeling the letdown of losing as much as any, opined that the best don't, after all, always win. Normally, he remembered to hold his tongue, his reactions being rejected by most, but he'd fallen prey to a false feeling of acceptance and oneness in this case. He had no more than said it when he was answered by Bob Wurstler, actually one of the boys Daniel sometimes imagined could be his friend. "Where is Penny to protect you, Chessler?" the redheaded young Wurstler taunted. "This is an American game, not an Indian or foreign game, like you would like."

The others simply looked away, like they always did.

The baseball-mad young fans in Newcastle School waited on the edge of their seats all morning the next Wednesday, October 6, to troop down for news of the fourth game, played at Exposition Park in Pittsburgh on the 5th, only to have Gammage send word up to them by courier that the game had been called on account of rain, and was being played instead that very afternoon.

But if the delay dampened anyone's spirits locally, they weren't letting on. The next day they tromped down the hundred steps in a jaunty mood, the now lifelong Boston fans among them secretly dreading the result. And, indeed, they learned by reading the dispatch off the wire that, due to the Boston Americans' sloppy play and bum luck, the Pirates had again triumphed, 5 to 4, to go up three games to one.

By contrast, the long procession down to the news office on Thursday had the feeling—as one of the students put it—of going to a hanging. If Boston had lost again in the fifth game, they were dead ducks for sure. One of the perennial troublemakers at the school, Ed Tokler—a Pittsburgh rooter, of course—indiscreetly followed up this observation by asking, "Which side is Diamond Slim on?" And someone else muttered to the effect that he'd probably "lost his head over it."

But, wonder of wonders! The Boston team put together its best effort to date, and won game five 11 to 2! Pittsburgh 3 games, Boston 2. Where there was life, there was still hope, Josh Russel, a freshman, summed it up.

Game 6 loomed like sudden death: If beloved Boston lost, the Series was over, and all was lost. If they won, then suddenly, the Series would be tied! But who could bear to read about it in news coming through a wire? "What if the sender got it wrong?" Jane Gooding wanted to know. "They don't get it wrong," Wurstler corrected her. "The telegrapher is at the games, I imagine."

Miracle of miracles! Observed in Newcastle a day afterward, on the morning of Friday, October 9: Game 6—Boston 6, Pittsburgh 3. The Series was tied! And students secretly bet their next six months' allowances on the outcome of what was left of it.

Now, Cy Young was to go up against Philippe, both proclaimed the greatest pitcher in America at different points in the Series.

On Saturday, it was learned by those lined up at the news office that Game 7, to have been played the day before, had been postponed due to unusually cold, windy conditions following a heavy rain overnight, and that a Saturday game was in question, too.

The school officials were getting antsy about continuing to permit the upper-grade students to leave the grounds together on any more days just to follow baseball, especially with training to defend the town still going on on the school's own athletic grounds. But precisely because the children were being deprived of their own field, it was decided to let them go ahead for another day or two to pursue their natural curiosity by making the trek.

On Monday, it was learned that "Deacon" Philippe, who had learned to play ball, it was said, on the remote prairie in South Dakota, lost the great pitching duel to Cy Young on Saturday in Pittsburgh, 7 to 3. Boston again led in the Series—which at the time was deemed to extend to best of nine games.

So the teams returned to Boston for a showdown game, to be played on Monday, the 12th, with one more final, follow-up game if necessary.

The dispatch the avid young fans in Newcastle read outside the news office on the subsequent Tuesday, a chilly and windy day across the Northern Plains, started off by extolling the players on the two teams for fraternizing like old chums when their trains met in Albany and traveling together the rest of the way. The more knowledgeable students perused the batting orders and succession of plays in all the games and imagined they heard the crack of the bat and the cheer or groan that went up after each bit of the unfolding drama. In this, people all over America lived in rapt unison for the two weeks consumed by the greatest Series, while virtually all other matters of concern were set aside. And now, it was all coming to a conclusion. The drama would finally (and too soon) be over, and the winner—though both sides and fandom everywhere were resounding winners—would be known.

At 2:30 on Monday, the teams had taken the field and the game began. At the end of the ninth, with Honus Wagner's last mightily slugged ball safely cradled in Lou Criger's mitt, the home-standing Boston Americans were ahead 3 to 0. And the great World Series—the first ever—was over.

Someone asked, as the Newcastle bunch veritably raced back up the hill, "You think there will be another Series next year? An older, wiser student answered him, "Probably, yes. But it won't be the first."

◄►

That night at home, Daniel told old Chessler all about the last game and how much he had enjoyed the jaunts down to follow the whole thing, and showed him the printed dispatch—which also had gone to all the saloons and stores downtown and the rooms in the hotel. And a prominent part was that President Roosevelt had praised the Series and the game.

Then, he shared how much he longed for acceptance at school and the camaraderie especially of the other boys. "I know it's all Martin's doing, our being ignored and left out. Pa, why do we stay here if we're not welcomed?"

"Daniel," Chessler began slowly, evenly, "if it weren't Martin here, it would likely be someone else like him elsewhere—with an intolerance for peace and fair-mindedness. Newcastle is our home as much as his, and we're not going to run away. We have nothing to be ashamed of. And we're not going to leave the source of a future in the bottom of a canyon for the likes of Martin to find. I know he was looking, when he was able to get around better. And he wasn't far from finding it, too—though, heaven knows, he doesn't need it now!

"No, we're not a threat to anyone," he continued. "And I don't believe there have been any Indians lurking around here, either. I think Martin just generated those reports and claims to spread fear and take more control, to flaunt his sickness for power. To sell more guns and bullets in his store, no doubt, even!"

Martina, Penny's little sister, stump-shaped and raven-haired, bounded into her grandfather's sitting room back in the deep interior of his castle-like Victorian home in the east part of town after school one day in October and sprawled across the old pistol's ample lap. A troubled girl, here was her only repose. In response, the bull uttered a sudden gasp, as if she'd forced him to exhale.

"How you is, little weasel?" he greeted her. "You are *so* like my sainted mother, in so many ways! The image of her..." And he wept.

"Me big and good and salty, old troll!" she squealed with delight. "Snake eggs!" she taunted, raking and goading him, laughing.

"And what you got for me?"

"Sandwich and honey!" she yelped, squealing out of control.

"Ok, well, then..." he provoked her with his stubby finger. And then he asked another question as part of their ritual, jerking her head back by pulling on one of her braids: "And what you got to *tell* me?"

"Oh, Grandpapa!" she pretended to sob. "It's Penny again, you know! I saw her at school, how she carries on with that *horrible* boy of Chessler's, kissing and fumbling every time they think no one's watching! Both of them low-down skunks..."

"Don't call her that, darling," he said. "Fumbling?"

"Yes, Grandpapa—you know!"

"Oh!" He smiled, and then looked aggrieved.

"...And, of Iris, your wonderful sainted aunt?" he asked her, rubbing his thumb over the smooth, pink skin that had grown over where her left index finger had been.

"Oh, Grandpapa," she implored, searching his earnest blue eyes, "can you give me a mountain lion for my own?"

"Ox won't like it. Think about it...We'll see. What about Iris?"

The old reprobate treated her routine sort of request with a fitting degree of seriousness. How could he help recalling that she'd gotten her own ox, staked at that very moment in her family's back yard, after begging for one of her own, just like a lumberman in some storybook, and saying she'd cut off her finger if she didn't get one. And then she followed through, explaining that when she'd held her breath and turned blue to get what she wanted, things still hadn't worked out.

"Yeah, Iris! You know what Aunt Iris is doing?" she asked him, pointedly.

"No, what is it she's doing, Angel?"

"She's been going up to that Chessler's pig-house where he lives, at night, and going on in there *with him.*"

Now, Martin *was* taken aback. "No!" he roared, threatening to wash out her mouth with sand if she ever dared say such a thing again. That was the last straw!

<><

A light rapping, sounding like a light rain, at the door signaled that Iris had used the cover of the deepest darkness that night for a visit. This, while half the town was in the bars for loud and endless rehashing and discussing of the Series, on which some had staked half their income or thousands in property.

Daniel opened back the heavy door and she came in and, passing the muster of a good sniff at the ankles by Red, went to unwrap and inspect Chessler's wounded leg at once. Finding it noticeably improved, she asked its owner an interesting question: "What is the rock you placed in my bag the last time I was here?"

"Rock? Oh! Why, that's a chunk of pure gold! Enough, I would say, to pay your bills for several months!"

She was taken aback. "Gold? In a coal town? I won't ask you where you got it. But what am I to do with it?"

"Good question! If there's someone you trust going to Rapid or Deadwood, or Cheyenne, send it along to be tested and cashed in. I can't tell you at the moment where it came from, and don't tell anyone hereabouts that you have it. Unless they're going to one of those places and you know for certain they are worthy of your trust."

Now, there came nothing less than a heavy *thud* on the outside of the door. And it seemed to swing wide open of its own accord. Two burly men raced in—one of them the swarthy Manfred, Martin's son, the other a near look-alike, both in beat-up looking top hats and unkempt beards. Their faces glowed red in the wavering, breeze-disturbed firelight.

Quick as thieves, Manfred grasped Iris under her arms and pulled her straight out the door, a vile name for her escaping his lips as an invective. The other man lunged at Chessler, catching him with his shoulder directly on the older man's wounded leg, the intent obviously being to thrash him to within an inch of his life, apparently assuming that Iris had come to visit him for illicit romantic purposes.

Daniel, a featherweight by comparison, was on the man's back in a trice, and it was Red at his throat that subdued him, with Chessler, still wincing, standing over and ready to crown him with a brass fire-poker. Together, the three of them lifted him up and threw him bodily out the door and then barred it.

"What'll they do to Iris?" Daniel fairly screamed.

"I don't reckon they'll hurt her," Chessler said, in a surprisingly even voice. "'Cause she's family, you know. Manfred is her brother-in-law. And Martin won't have an open scandal, I don't think, in his brood—at least his own as he sees it."

"And so, what do you think they surmise?" Daniel asked, fear still present in his voice.

"The worst," Chessler answered. "The absolute worst—for that's all they know."

And they both knew what that must mean for them. Daniel, in silence, finished dressing and re-wrapping his pa's leg.

The hardy old pioneer tossed in his lonely cob-stuffed bed most of that night trying to think of a way of throwing sand in Martin's deadly, laughable operation and his eyes, as he had done back in the bad days of their common youth, by disabling the cannon and warning his friends. But, if he took action, it would have to somehow be without getting himself killed and casting Daniel into an orphanage. As hard as he thought and as much as he dreamed of it, he was unable to hit on a likely way.

18

FULL MOON HUNT

After dawn on Friday, October 17, it turned unseasonably cold and snowy in Newcastle, with a whistling wind piling up drifts of tiny newly fallen hard granules all over the town and immediate vicinity. School was held, but few students made it up the icy steps that morning, and those who did, including Daniel Edgemont, sat huddled in their heavy woolen coats, gloves, and scarves, in wonder that the Indian summer they had enjoyed over the past several weeks had vanished so quickly and utterly.

For reasons of its own, the Lakota hunting party, crossing boldly into Wyoming where its members knew they wouldn't be welcomed by the current occupants, split into two groups. Six bucks and six squaws traveled south just over the border. The rest, twenty-three bucks and forty squaws and babes in arms, with a dozen decrepit wagons, headed west into the Thunder Basin country, plugging a slew of antelope and, reportedly, more than a few range cattle on the way—exactly as the whites had come in at the beginning and helped themselves and more to *their* cattle. And the days out on the prairie, by contrast, continued remarkably sun-drenched, almost balmy, with just a hint of a tang in the fall air in the mornings.

Some in the larger traveling group had never seen their prized ancestral hunting ground before, and so they did some touring. They traveled up to see the great tower of the devils at the north. They ascended the Sun Dance Mountain of legend and did the sun dance ceremony to call the spirit of the buffalo atop its broad summit, from which they could see to the corners of the world. They stood in a long line along the top of a ridge and trembled to see and feel the earth shake at the passage of the disheartening iron horse cutting the land in two.

They came upon and explored the moldering ruins of the once-feared and hated old Fort Fetterman, some distance north of the Platte, which had been abandoned for more than two decades now. Truly, few in this party had ever ventured far from home, Pine Ridge. They found the sage brush and tufts of grass promiscuously mixed with the pines and aspen, golden in the fall and topping all the buttes, and the mocking birds amidst groves of willow in the low stream beds. And a thing they didn't expect they didn't see—or saw only in visions in their minds—the thousands upon thousands upon thousands of buffalo of the old ones.

The outermost ranch people watched their progress and charted their movement. They stopped on the trail when entering at the border from Dakota at a little isolated farm beside Cold Springs Creek, and one of the men, Iron Shield, admired the fine facial features in miniature of the little girl Clara Hon, three years old, standing only up to his thigh, but unafraid as she knelt to hand him a cup of water, her rustic parents watching with pride. He knew there was good in these people. And the others the party they approached at their doors and in their houses were no less generous in actions, their hands perhaps stopped by fear. Only twice were rifles seen, held in abeyance, held back doubtless by the numbers.

"These are not fearsome people," Iron Shield spoke to Eagle Feather/Charlie Smith.

And he agreed, "Singly, they are not all devils."

One brave, called Yellow Eyes, unkempt, a bit older and considered eccentric, traveled off a distance to the right side of the moving party generally, at times bringing the first news of a thing encountered. In early afternoon on October 18, Yellow Eyes came on foot, leading his horse, almost running to tell of something he had observed.

"What have you seen now, Yellow Eyes?" Eagle Feather /Charlie Smith asked him, a certain lack of respect apparent in his tone.

Yellow Eyes, undaunted, answered: "Buffalo. I saw an old bull walking on the far ridge to the right."

"I suppose it was a white man's cow," High Bull commented, and the others nodded and murmured.

"I saw a buffalo," Yellow Eyes said, holding his ground. He leaped onto the back of his horse and bade the others to follow, and several did, for a short trot toward the ridge a mile to the west. Yellow Eyes reined up and stopped near the foot of the steep incline leading up to the top, still half a mile from the summit. Extending his arm, he pointed. And, surprising to all, an old, shaggy, gray-coated bull buffalo stood facing them for a long time, assessing, and then turned and moved farther away.

The little band of six or seven then let out a whoop and galloped at full speed in the direction of the amazingly rare beast, each one wanting the honor of bringing it down. To do so would be both an omen and the rarest prize—which all of them felt cheated of before that time.

Racing pell-mell to the top of the ridge, all were shocked to behold there was no buffalo to be found anywhere in the bowl-shaped valley or atop its surrounding rim. The old lone animal had disappeared, leaving only the wind to betoken his presence before.

Every day for the next five days, the lone old buffalo was seen on a hilltop or ridge up ahead, and though everyone strained to hurry on and riders advanced ahead to reach it, when the turf the animal had occupied was reached, there was no sign. On the third day, Iron Shield went to the place in his wagon where Chief Red Cloud had placed a ramshackle *camera obscura* he had gotten someplace, an ancient model, and hauled it out and, according to Red Cloud's directions, made an image on glass of the old bison standing against the distant sky to offer proof back at Pine Ridge.

◄►

Word of Indians in numbers—100 and 200 out and about were bandied commonly—hit Newcastle like a shot.

Martin called a meeting of the Wyoming Volunteer Regiment at the school sports field on October 19th, a snowy day in Newcastle. More than three hundred attended, according to some accounts. Others said five hundred. Sheriff Miller and all the deputies showed up uninvited, to "coordinate," as the sheriff put it, with Martin, who was styling himself "Colonel."

"Martin," Sheriff Miller said to him, "I get the impression that you actually want a scrap. Would that be true?"

"Yeah," the old scamp answered, grinning just a bit, hands plunged into his pockets like a kid caught peeking up a girl's dress. "I mean, all this practicing and preparation...Well, what would you expect? All of us! We are ready! Bring 'em on!"

"But I'm here to assure you—the lot of you—," Sheriff Miller responded, "that I and my deputies are going to be taking care of this problem, as we did in the past. That's what you asked me to stand for sheriff of Weston County to do, and that's what I will do—primarily, with the help of my trained and sworn deputies. And if we need more men for a posse, we will gratefully contact you at that time and deputize more men for the occasion."

"But can you wipe out those savages once and for all and rid the country of all of them, Mr. Sheriff? Eliminate them?" Martin pilloried him.

"Well, no, we won't do that," said Miller, "that's not what we're about, exactly.

You see, we don't hate Indians. And we don't want anybody getting killed. In fact, what we want is to *prevent* that. That's our sworn job." He stopped and waited for that discordant message to sink in and draw a response, then he continued. "I've been approached to form a posse to arrest the alleged transgressors of our game laws. It's not a killin' offense."

"Alleged? Transgressors of game laws?" an unidentified man in the back of those assembled shouted. "You callin' shootin' cattle 'alleged'?"

"Yes, sir, I am! We're not plannin' to kill any Indians. They're not here to attack us, but to go on a fall hunting excursion in a part of the country that used to be theirs for a lot o' generations before we showed up! At least, that's how they look at it!"

"*Gooooooooo!* You ain't goin' soft on us are you, Sheriff?" Bailey, the sweaty-handed jeweler and locksmith asked him.

"No, I'm not," the sheriff answered him evenly, "but I was hired—elected— hired by all of you to uphold the law and to maintain justice, not to wage warfare! *That's* long in the past now! That's not why these reservation Sioux are here! In the main, these Indians are friendly and reasonable, as long as we treat them fair! And most of them weren't even born when all the battles you remember, and some of you no doubt took part in, I suppose, were happening!

"And, if we, or you, were to go out and shoot them, it would be considered murder. And you could potentially hang for it!"

"Come on, Sheriff, hang for wastin' a worthless Injun?" It was the same fellow in the back again. "Let me tell you sometime what they done to my two brothers, back some time now!"

"What? When was that?"

"Well, it was in the 1870s. And that's how we know what murderous treachery they're capable of! And, we, Americans, we're the *good* people, don't ever lose sight of that, Sheriff!"

"Well, let's put it this way," Billy Miller responded. "The people can vote me out as sheriff if they're not happy with the way I do my job. But I'm tellin' you this—if anyone not legally constituted and sworn goes out to do harm to anyone outside the laws of this state and county, I personally will arrest them—same as Indians who are breaking the game laws. And don't be too surprised if you end up sharin' a jail cell with them!"

He stopped again, to let what he'd said sink in. Then, he spoke again. (In fact, he spoke more now than anyone could remember him ever having spoken about anything.) "In the unlikely event that any Indians come into town with hostility in mind, or try, really and genuinely, to do damage to persons or property here, then you all will have a place in my plans. But until or unless that happens, which I don't think it will, you can all butt out now and go back to your homes!"

Having unburdened himself, finally, he mounted his prized horse, Surprise, and, followed by his four deputies, including Deputy John Owens, rode back to the office in part of his comfortable home alongside the jail to confer with them.

At that little conclave, Deputy Owens in particular bit his lip and bided his time before attempting to offer counsel. The net result up to now, he knew, had not been promising or positive. The few doubters that he had convinced there was no Indian threat, were now thinking again that Martin was right and wise!

Some of the Lakota in the split travel troupe—including a brave named High Dog—had been present on the spring of 1901 excursion, when Sheriff Billy Miller had arrested the alleged miscreants and confiscated their horses to pay fines and to compensate ranchers whose cattle had allegedly been harvested. Jack Red Cloud, the old renowned chief's son, had been among those allegedly persecuted on earlier travel permit warranted trips into Wyoming. Eagle Feather/Charlie Smith in particular continued percolating on high boil over the fact the Sioux, as primordial lords of the land, weren't welcomed and accommodated on these nostalgic revisits.

And he, as designated co-leader of the troupe on this visit, together with his half-breed friend William Brown, vowed that he would not be taken into Newcastle by the despised sheriff, even if it meant shooting him. The white men, who flaunted the Indians' established laws and killed all their cattle, and the white man's laws could all go hang.

On October 24 or early on the 25th, Sheriff Miller and his special deputized posse of nine hand-picked men ran into the smaller Sioux contingent (six men and six squaws) near Lance Creek, a day's ride south of Newcastle. Miller sent three of the deputies back with the twelve Indians to hold them in jail, while he and the five others rode west to head off the larger contingent in Thunder Basin, trailing them until the following Friday, the 30th.

On the dry fork of the Cheyenne River, they found them, encamped with their dozen ramshackle wagons—23 bucks and 40 squaws and papooses under Eagle Feather/Smith and William Brown.

Brown's squaw, an open and friendly woman and would-be friend of the sheriff, whom she knew, rustled up some victuals at once for these fellow travelers.

About an hour later, Charlie Smith/Eagle Feather rode in, and Sheriff Miller immediately read his arrest warrant to him. Smith/Feather asked the sheriff to hold on until William Brown came in, which he did, whooping and yelling along with others as they rode down over the ridge.

Eagle Feather then denied the charges that they had shot antelope, claiming they had traded for the three in their possession.

"If that's true, you'll find you won't have any troubles with authorities in Newcastle," Miller answered evenly.

William Brown said he would go into Newcastle to face charges. But Eagle Feather said he knew the white man's law, and wasn't going.

The Sioux, as well as the Sheriff's party, were heavily armed, making the standoff edgy.

Eagle Feather/Smith signaled with a wave of his arm to others to come along with him, then mounted and started out due east.

"That's not the way to Newcastle," Sheriff Miller said.

"I don't live in Newcastle!" the headstrong Carlisle graduate answered him.

Miller then rode over to Brown, who reiterated he was ready to cooperate. But Smith/Eagle Feather was riding away, and others were trying to decide what to do.

Sheriff Billy Miller, finding his little band uncomfortably surrounded, quickly realized he didn't have enough strength or threat of firepower to arrest this increasingly uncooperative party. Accordingly, leaving two men to trail and keep an eye on the Indians, he headed back to Newcastle for reinforcements, to return in strength the next day.

As he and his companions disappeared over the hill to the north, the other Indians were hitching up the wagons to follow their more decisive leader back toward Pine Ridge and home.

◄►

Pandemonium appeared to have struck the Miller household in Newcastle. That night, October 30, Anna herself was occupied packing and repacking for the twelfth time for a little trip over into western South Dakota on long-anticipated business of her own, buying clothes and catching her breath a bit. Now, she was kept busy reassuring the younger children—especially the little boys, Sidney and Raymond—that Daddy would be okay and could take care of himself if he ran into the Indians they had heard were around. The boys, with the help of four-year-old Ruth, were supposedly working under the supervision of older sister Mary to carve a pumpkin for the Halloween party to be held at the school the next night, which happened to be Saturday.

Billy had appeared at the door briefly late that afternoon, while the children were still on their way home, for a kiss and a change of clothes before putting out the call for more men to leave on an overnight ride back to the southwest. But Anna had already stepped out and missed him.

The weather had turned mild and almost summer-like.

19

THE BATTLE OF LIGHTNING CREEK

Heading back out on Surprise, Sheriff Miller rendezvoused with six more men, the last that he deputized, while traveling through the Fiddleback gate route to Thunder Basin, southwest of Newcastle. Among these was Johnny Owens, who had been summoned earlier.

As soon as the braves came into view, Owens, riding up front with Billy Miller, said to him clearly, in the hearing of all, "There's your Indians, Sheriff."

The two of them rode together up the intervening bank, and Miller shouted out to the Indian riders, holding up his hand, "I have to arrest you! Please surrender and make this as easy as we can!" The Indians dismounted and the posse stepped into the cover of a copse of trees.

Miller spoke in a calm voice to his men, "No shooting at all, leastwise until I give the word." He then began to steadily and repeatedly call out to the conflicted Sioux, in a loud voice, urging them to surrender and lower their guns. When his voice began to break, he asked Owens to call out, and the chief deputy did so, until he, too, grew too hoarse.

A rifle shot then cracked above Johnny Owens's now rusty hinge of a voice. Owens went on readying his guns, not realizing that Sheriff Miller had fallen beside him with a shot to the groin.

A few yards away, Louis Falkenberg, one of the deputies, died instantly from a bullet through the neck.

Owens and some of the others, dodging bullets, carried Sheriff Billy Miller to a nearby cabin, where he died within half an hour from loss of blood that couldn't be stopped. Owens had kept blasting away with his gun and another one handed to him steadily while they bore their forlorn leader away.

Meanwhile, Black Kettle, one of the more indignant of the Lakota, was killed almost instantaneously, and later, some identified him as the one who had shot first. Eagle Feather/Smith bled to death after being hit in the legs. And two others of their party died in the fighting.

William Brown, wanting no part of any of it, set out for Pine Ridge at the very start of hostilities.

Mrs. Eagle Feather was also wounded in the fighting.

◀▷

News of the fierce firefight quickly reached Newcastle, Lusk to the south, and Douglas to the west, and posses quickly converged. Nine fleeing Sioux were overtaken heading east, just over the border in South Dakota, and since it was surmised that the battle had actually taken place in Converse County, the prisoners were taken and held in the Douglas jail awaiting trial for murder of peace officers, District Judge Garland Daniels presiding.

As soon as he received word of the battle by telegraph, Governor Fennemore Chatterton, down in Cheyenne, determined that the Indians implicated in the shootings must hang, in order to serve as a clear example to all of the wages of lawlessness in a state that still could go either way. Chatterton, a Republican, was reviled by many for not commuting the death sentence of Tom Horn, a generally-lawful reputed assassin and popular hero convicted of murder on weak evidence. But in this case, he knew he was on safe ground politically. Not one to trifle with, the Governor warned Judge Daniels rather ominously that if these Indians didn't pay, things might not go well for him. Which either meant that the irate populace could be expected to exact revenge, or else forces unspecified, including the Governor, might.

Judge Daniels kept his own counsel. Indeed, there was a rumor that, because he didn't bother to answer the Governor's telegram—whether he in fact did or didn't—the Governor was pulling strings to have him replaced prior to the trial.

The mob in Newcastle—composed, it was said by local observers, largely of the same mostly-faceless outsiders that had hung Diamond L. Slim—once again surrounded the jail in Newcastle on November 2, supposing that the Indian prisoners must have been secreted there in the night. The Miller children were moved out by family friends who were overseeing in both their parents' absence, to protect them from the rumored impending incursion and torching of the building.

Anna was tracked down and informed in Rapid City, where she'd just checked into a hotel, but not done any hobnobbing or made any purchases yet. It took her a long, painful day to make her way back home.

Indeed, residents of Newcastle and Weston County, and of most all of Wyoming, overwhelmingly demanded revenge and a hard lesson to be taught to outside Indians, who would surely come as marauders at will, it was frequently said, should the young pioneer communities show leniency now. "What is Red Cloud up to?" became a ubiquitous question without an answer. "We've got to teach these savages that they have no place in our civilized state," most everyone repeated, "that they can't break our game laws and assault our peace officers and get away with it. I say we send a message back to Red Cloud—maybe arrest him, too—and hang them all."

The eight charged were held under secure guard in Douglas in the Converse County jail, eighty miles from Newcastle. There was talk in the air about making an assault on that lockup, to prevent legal shenanigans from getting the guilty parties off. This was followed by a stern warning issued jointly by the interim Weston County sheriff, Fred Coates, and the Converse County sheriff, that this time, tampering with the law would be treated strictly as obstruction of justice and prosecuted. Editorials in the *News-Journal*, in *Bill Barlow's Budget* in Douglas, and in papers all over the state and the western country thundered against the Lakota Sioux who couldn't let bygones be and had invaded a well-intentioned and peaceful community—*in the twentieth century!*

The eight defendants were registered in Douglas as Iron Shield, Chief He Grow, Red Pin, High Bull, Broken Nose, High Dog, James White Elk, Charge Wolf, and Jessie Little War Bonnet. Their leaders and several of their fellows were gone—either killed in the battle or vamoosed back to the reservation, and no serious attempt was made to bring any of the other participants back to face charges. Meanwhile, Major Brennan, the superintendent at Pine Ridge, made the trip over to encourage his fallen wards, who also had, in U.S. District Attorney Burke, up from Cheyenne, an appointed defense counsel.

Acting Sheriff Coates had been appointed over the objections of many of Deputy Owens's supporters, and was obviously not cognizant of some things in the town. He settled, nonetheless, upon an ingenious method of getting word of the daily proceedings in Douglas back to the highly animated and waiting citizens of Newcastle as quickly as possible. Word was to be telephoned over from the Douglas court house to the one phone box in Newcastle, at the lower end of Main Street. Old Chessler, the familiar custodian of most of the churches, was commissioned to wait there in the cold for the incoming call. Then, he was to go and ring the bell in the tower of the Methodist Episcopal Church, well down the west slope of the town, loud and clear—*once* if the defendants had been found guilty, *twice* if found innocent, and *thrice* if the proceedings had been carried over into the following day.

Talk ran rampant in Newcastle's saloons and shops, workplaces, and probably around all of the city's dinner tables through all the days from the funerals and burials of the two beloved peace officers, until the day set for the opening of the court hearing, November 7. It seemed that nothing else was on anyone's mind.

Most supposed that Governor Chatterton's pronouncements and widely-rumored threats of intrigue or open action against the judge, should he stray from his clear duty, would assure a guilty ruling. Meanwhile, tales circulated about Judge Daniels's bizarre habits and beliefs—although no one in Newcastle seemed to actually know him or know anything about him firsthand. Still, most somehow felt that the law, as practiced or "interpreted" as it was called by lawyers and judges, had little or nothing to do with the brand of justice meted out by sheriffs and marshals—which was what made the towns of the West at least halfway safe places of abode at least part of the time.

So, when judges and lawyers, attorneys and the like got involved in things, who could know how things might turn out? It was a turkey shoot to be sure, that's all that could be said.

And some even said that if that Judge Daniels fellow were to let those marauding Indian terrorizers off, well, then, they ought to go after *him* as a menace to the community. But then, surely, he wouldn't defy the Governor, nor the letters and declarations of their own Congressman from Newcastle, Mr. Mondell. Although they didn't know Judge Daniels, surely he wouldn't be *that* stupid!

When November 7 came, County Attorney Mecum of Douglas presented testimony by eight members of the posse to the effect that peace officers Miller and Owens had repeatedly shouted out to the defendants, warning them that they must surrender, and that no member of the special posse had fired until an Indian did.

District Attorney Burke offered no defense at all, and none of the defendants—who were not United States citizens at that point—spoke.

Judge Daniels deliberated briefly and consulted with some officers of the court, and then ruled.

20

BELLS!

A cold front came in on the morning of November 7, bringing to Newcastle plummeting temperatures and freezing rain combined with sleet. Conditions worsened as the daylight died.

Daniel and Chessler, with Red, had spent the forenoon out at the water station by the canyon and the old road, and Chessler had managed one descent and return strenuously lugging a dirt-encrusted gold bar up to the cabin before the storm closed in and sent them heading through the gathering gloom and gale toward home. Huddled up next to his pa in the wagon under the tarp they shared for warmth, Daniel made the sort of observation that made old Chessler particularly proud of him. "Pa," he said through chattering teeth, "why is it that the mild and good always suffer for the harsh and extreme?" He was obviously thinking of Sheriff Miller, as thoroughly good a man as either of them knew, and possibly also of John and Luella.

"Son, I reckon it must be just set in the pattern of the world some way. It's no accident, we both know that."

"You reckon Sheriff Miller's in a better place?"

"Well, I don't know but what he's in the same place," Chessler said. "Maybe just a bit higher, like maybe a foot, and set to a different tune or thought is all."

"And what you thinkin' those Indians will get?"

"Oh, I don't know—maybe a good tongue-lashin' when they get back to Pine Ridge. Maybe somethin' a whole lot worse! All I know is, I'm liable to be the first man in Newcastle to know, ain't I?" He grinned and winked at his boy, to show that everything would be all right for them, even if their world would end and the whole town turned and came savagely after them, something they'd had occasion to halfway expect for some time. Nurturing fear, though, didn't serve one despised for being out of step.

As the day passed and darkened, anticipation mounted throughout the county and town, particularly in the dives and saloons, where the men and an occasional brazen damsel held forth on the crime of the moment as gathered from the series of news bulletins everyone had swallowed and on the fiends, or "terrorizers," as they were being called of late, in the reports. All such as they needed to be smashed, obliterated, yanked into eternity at the end of eight side-by-side ropes. And the niceties of the law must not be permitted to blot out justice for them. Nor would they, by gum! What other interpretation could be reached by Christian men with families?

For, who had fired shots first? That much was not in dispute. Nor, then, was the sensible verdict, directed, the citizenry supposed, by simple eyesight, decency, common sense.

But, would it be so? There was still that question. Anyone listening for long in the hollows of the Antlers Hotel back rooms or even the House of Blazes would detect a troubled uncertainty in all the endless talk, some note of lingering doubt among the staunchly unanimous patrons as to how the verdict actually *would* go when it came down from Olympus.

All knew the code of signals, the different bell tolls and what to expect, and the crowd inside quieted to a hush to hear amid the intensifying smoke in each of the hellholes as the hour finally approached.

And they waited. Four o'clock. Four-thirty. Five. They continued to wait, more anxious with the passing hours.

And Daniel, huddled in his sheepskin on the steps of the library, to be sure to be within range to hear, waited. Silence. Silence still. Waiting and freezing, his coat adhering to the iron railing, hands tingling, burning, stiffening.

At six o'clock by the Court House clock, he rose, and brushing away a deepening rime of pellets frozen to his leather front, he prized his bicycle tires free from the freezing ground and glided off bumping into the night blackness, bumping, bumping, block by block out toward the west end of Newcastle to see whatever could have happened to delay the message.

Arriving at the M.E. Church, which he saw through the viscous frosty atmosphere in vague silhouette, its bulk hidden behind a thick veil of swirling sleet and fog in the darkness, Daniel got off his bicycle and walked it all the way up the long path to the door of the ghostlike stone building without detecting the least sign of life. He stood there shivering, rocking forward and back on his frozen feet, his face on fire, for a long moment. Gazing into the stinging maelstrom, sweeping his blinded gaze in all directions, he at length perceived a muffled voice that he first took to be a hinge somewhere blowing freely in the wind. "Daniel, I'm down here," he heard, the far-away voice calm but at the same time pleading. Traipsing around in widening circles, he found it came from his own pa, Old Chessler, slumped there on the ground under the steeple.

"Pa! What's happened to you?" he inquired in a voice so poignant and fine it could have been a real angel's.

"The rung of the ladder up there inside the steeple gave way," his pa said, recalling as he said it that it had always been perfectly sound and sturdy before. "I guess I must a fell in a heap here, and when nobody came by, I must o' fallen to sleep right here on the ground."

"Are you bad hurt?" Daniel asked.

"I don't know," the old man answered. "I don't think so. It was quite a thud, though, and my leg—the sore one—is bent under me sort of funny, and I'm sure I'll be stiff and sore at least. But, I honestly don't know if I'm bad hurt for sure or not."

Daniel could see him a little now, sitting up.

"But, one thing's for sure—there's no ringin' the bell o' this church, 'cause they ain't no way a anybody getting' up to it!"

He sat and thought for a minute and just sighed. Then, he said, "See, Daniel, that judge in Douglas let them Indians go! 'Cause he said there wasn't any evidence a who might a fired shots and who didn't. So, if one o' them was guilty, there was no way he could know it or which one...or which two. That's what that call said from Douglas. It was one of the posse members from here that called."

"So he turned them all loose?"

"Yeah! Released the whole lot to the Indian agent to see they all got taken straight on home.

"Now then, Daniel," he resumed, "I want you to git back on that contraption o' yours and ride out there up the hill to that old church you used to play around out there to the west, that one we called 'Old Castle,' remember? The bell's still good up in that steeple—you remember, sometimes we could hear it ringin' there blowed around in the night! And there's a stiff rope hangin' down to the ground from it. I want you to go and pull that rope and ring the bell just as loud and clear as you can—*twice*. And they all should hear it clear to downtown. It won't be as loud, but they should hear it!"

Daniel thought for a few seconds on this. "Well, but what about you?" he asked.

"Don't worry, boy, old Jerry's staked to that tree over there, waiting all this time." He slowly and cautiously stood up, with a helping hand, a little bent, but apparently no more than shaken up pretty good by his fall. "So I'll make it home okay—and get the fire goin' and maybe find somethin' to eat by the time you show up!"

Daniel started out again into the night, riding of necessity almost too slow to keep his bike balanced in the deepening slush and fighting the sharp headwind up the long, narrow, winding path to the top of the distant hill, guided mostly by feel. He rode on for a good hour, pumping hard to the crest of the hill where the old, partial wreck of a church loomed heavenward, and found the rope, stiff as a grape vine and two inches thick, and pulled it down with his whole weight. Once...twice.

Downtown, the saloons seemed eerie—smoke-filled and full to the gills, yet quiet as a church at four a.m. For hours, everyone kept waiting like that for the signal, now long overdue. All the drinking dives were the same. If anyone tried to talk, they were quickly shushed by the others with a hostile glare. And if their patrons all could have held their collective breath for that long, they would have done it.

"Whatever could have happened?" everybody thought—meaning with the trial in Douglas and with the dimly-viewed commissioned ringer and the awaited bell as well—the thought loud enough in everyone's mind, you would swear you'd heard it spoken.

Drinks were tossed back and reordered with hardly the clink of a glass, the re-ordering done by pointing, with everyone listening, listening, listening.

And then, faintly, as though from miles away in the storm-blasted night— "Bong!" just barely audible, and smiles crossed a thousand faces. "Just one!"..."- Bong!" again. The smiles were replaced by looks of consternation, confoundment, concern,...waiting for the third to come. Silence.

Then, they all started to talk, low at first, then increasing in volume slowly to the usual midnight din, glasses clinking. But without the laughter. Someone said they thought the wind had blown away the third and final expected "bong."

Everyone sighed, and hoped, awaiting further word.

21

HOW THE CHANGE FINALLY CAME

Sunday morning, November 8, dawned clear and still, with a fresh, thick blanket of powder snow covering the ground. That day passed deceptively quiet, as people kept to their houses or went to church and the feel of the town was numb and drowsy, all the principals drained and worn out—some hung over—from the tension and confusion of the night before. The mood in Newcastle was like a spring-load mechanism that hadn't yet been cocked or engaged. And so it was that the day faded uneasily into night.

On Monday morning, when Bobby Gammage, the editor of the *News-Journal*, arrived for work at 7:30, the sun was just peeking over the horizon, and already, men were lined up out to Main Street, anxious for clarification of the enigmatic signal—apparently, two far-off clangs of a bell—they had received on Saturday night. There were posse members back from Douglas, but they had wisely declined to explain what had occurred in the courtroom.

Gammage once again printed up sheets to hand out from what had come over the wire—just as he had done with the championship baseball series results. But this was for real! Something fervently cared about and close to home! The men stood stock-still, shivering in the early light, their hands extended to receive and cradle the sheets as he passed down the line quickly, saying nothing.

It seemed as if they were all beholding and taking in the tidings as one, at exactly the same instant, and the first response from anyone was a surprised whistle. "Well, that mother _____," someone intoned lowly. "Well, I'll be, he really *was* that dumb!" another gave in a higher-pitched whine of a voice, and chuckled humorlessly, while others just grunted and stomped off alone to their workplaces, public houses, and homes.

A fuse, it seemed, had been lit. Would it burn itself out?

◄►

John Owens, with an apron on in the kitchen of his establishment, cooking up pancakes within minutes for some of the same individuals who had just been in the line in front of the *News-Journal*, was trying to figure out which way the pent up energy would flow now. Would the animus coalesce and lash out as before? Was there a sinister force that would assemble and use these automatons as pawns, as he feared? Would the town settle back down, or would it strike at its presumed enemies? He looked and listened intently as he went out to serve the customers. And regardless of the direction the release of energy took, he surmised he was going to have to act to defuse the real problem.

He cleared the breakfast dishes and washed them in his big wash tub in the back, with suds up to his elbows, dried off, and then went to have a talk with Fred Coates, the interim Sheriff. An hour later, at 10:30, both men emerged, Coates saddling up and heading east with a posse he had hastily assembled from the dozen men on standby, and Owens more circumspectly heading on foot for an address down in the east part of town.

◀▶

Chessler and Daniel used the calm afternoon that day to resume the work at their special excavation at the canyon and cabin, even though it had turned cold. The moment they arrived, old Chessler found that something was amiss. Checking as always to make sure everything was secure, he found that his most prized possession—his buffalo gun he'd owned for thirty years—was missing from the strongbox under the loose floor boards of the skeletal old structure. And whoever had found that would have to know about the growing cache of gold bars secreted there.

Daniel, looking over toward him and seeing his sober paleness and sudden loss of animation, instantly thought that he had suffered some kind of bodily attack. Indeed, his Pa couldn't speak: he just pointed down into the open space under the lifted boards. And then they looked at each other open-mouthed, lost for words.

Instinctively, Daniel stepped back outside and looked around, toward the crude road in front, and in back in the direction of the creek and canyon. And saw a large figure moving through the spaces between the now-bare trees toward them, crunching leaves. "Pa!" he warned, not loud.

Standing together peering out the open doorframe, they saw it was Martin, the old blunderer, disheveled and ragged as always, bearing the heavy, distinctively shortened Hawken rifle, coming toward them with an almost mirthful look.

Martin, appearing now as an unstoppable juggernaut, having all the force on his side, stopped, leveled and steadied the barrel of the gun, and fired with a resounding crack—and missed! The shell lodged in the wood of the doorframe, inches from old Chessler's exposed head.

Then, apparently surprised at having missed, he methodically reloaded and leveled the gun again, seemingly unmindful of Red lunging straight for his ankles.

While Daniel and Chessler stood looking at each other, mouths open in terror, he slowly drew a bead, this time, it seemed, at Chessler's heart. And then, drunk apparently, he started to sway forward and back, just catching himself from losing his balance and falling headlong, and staggered to regain his stance. Slowly, once again, he drew a bead.

And a gun roared—but it wasn't the Hawken. The sound came from behind, and, at once, the heavy buffalo gun fell to the ground and Martin's unsteady hands flailed upward, splurting blood.

The rescue shooter was presently seen to be Johnny Owens, who had trailed Martin to this spot, and grazed his right-hand knuckles with a precise shot. He stepped out from the trees, and Martin, still flailing his hand, wheeled around to face him.

"Owens! Jackal!" his timid stammering now roared.

"Martin, you old coot, you're the author of all this misery hereabouts!" Owens said. "And I'm puttin' you away!"

"Johnny Owens, Jack Slade's old partner!" Martin started laughing rather like a jackal himself, or a hyena.

"Slade?"

"Yeah, Slade, and his hired man on the stage line, Hickok. And remember how you and Hickok that one night in the bar in Sidney took turns splitting those hombres' scalps with bullets, just because they made fun of Hickok's hairstyle?"

Owens looked mortified. "No, Martin," he said, clearly taken aback. "I wasn't there!"

Even Chessler and Daniel had to wonder if he wasn't, somehow.

"And now, you, like Chessler here, and his old man—remember him, back at the fort?—have been soft on Injuns. Why Chessler here'd like to know how you and Slade nailed Injuns you caught waylaying stages to fence rails an' left them to either freeze or dry out in the sun. And..."

"No! I never had anything to do with that bastard! A good man, maybe one day a month, a rotten killer the rest...No, it's not true!"

Chessler, coming back to himself, had never realized how much a man of Johnny Owens's remarkable gun skills and steel temperament had had through the years to maintain an aura of virtue.

Obviously, though, Owens and Martin—just like Old Chessler and Martin—went way back.

"The Sheriff, Mr. Coates, isn't going to back you up, Owens," Martin remarked, confidently playing his ace, "because I made him the sheriff!"

"Oh, that's where you're wrong," John Owens answered his cunning, but now neutered nemesis. "I had a talk with him before I came out. Your terrorist days are done!"

"Well, we'll see...when those horrible savages get the hangin' that's comin' to 'em, before they ever reach the Dakota line! People are goin' to be grateful to the old Regiment then!"

"Nope, you stupid asp," Owens said, having clearly regained his aplomb. "Sheriff Fred and an honest posse big enough are probably waylaying your regiment of slaves and fools as I speak!"

"So, what you gonta charge me for? I've uncovered the biggest gold heist in the Wyoming Territory days right here and captured the wrongful benefactor at that!"

"Nope, Marty, I know he's been recoverin' it for a long time, and he's entitled to it for findin' it at this late date—the insurance has paid it off a long time ago! And he and his fine son he's raised sure needs it, after the job you did on 'em all these years!

"And that ain't all, either! I been followin' you up and investigating you for a long time, too! And just now, I'm able to do sumpthin' about it! You had a good man there in Billy Miller as your sheriff! But, he didn't have the stomach to unravel you and heal up what's really been wrong with this fine town and county. I know about all the inside jobs you've pulled around here, makin' it look like outsiders or Indians, or the angry people—people you made angry and fearful—was responsible for! I investigated each and every one of those insider jobs, and just waited, biding my time, with the evidence—until now!"

Martin looked bewildered. "Okay, well, if I'm gone, who's gonna run my businesses and sign all the checks and arrange all the rental office and mining and banking stuff, and retail, and whatever else around here? And take care of my poor invalid wife?"

Johnny Owens flashed a grin at this query—not nonsensical because Martin's enterprises and properties were probably most of the economy of the county—obviously just waiting for him to ask.

"Well, we'll get Manfred declared incompetent first thing—any judge we asked would gladly rule that way, I'm thinkin'. And that would leave—well, Iris! Iris! The good woman you've abused and, *she tells me now, just today*—and dare I say it?—*raped* all these several years since you arranged to have your good, sound son murdered! That finally made my mind up to act *today*—and damned glad it did! You got lots of murders on your hands, now, don't you? I think we can prove a dozen or so—all done by your stinking cat's paws, up to now. Not to mention the cowards afraid of their own shadows who knew and just went along, some of whom could be your cellmates! *If* you're lucky enough not to hang. Being crazy might just keep you away from that predicament!

"And, while we're at it," he added, "it's always been beyond me why those Lakota from over there, or whatever of them wanted to, couldn't come back and have a hunt, so long as they was told and followed the rules, just like anyone else!"

Then, he turned and spoke to Chessler. "Mighty fine boy you've got there, old man! And I know about your situation with your leg, too!"

Chessler shot him a quizzical look.

"Right!" he continued. "Iris told me everything! Now, you'll be able to visit her and get the attention you need for it, right at the hospital. And she can come and visit you, like she wants to, out in the open—as your friend!" And he looked over to Daniel, too. "And bring Penny along on out, too, whenever she wants to come."

He paused. "And you can use some of that gold stashed away to build you a proper house and even send the boy to Laramie, or Cornell, or wherever he wants to go, for college. We've got to safeguard that hoard of gold you got better, though. I've known you were onto it for years, but couldn't do a thing to help without being conspicuous." He smiled wistfully. "Ya see, I knew just about where it had to be, but could never touch it myself without raisin' suspicions I was in on the robbery!"

Without further ado, this man so full of wonders and surprises strode over to his horse, out of sight back in the trees, training his pistol back effortlessly on the beclouded Martin the whole time, and drew a strong net out of his saddle bag. This he cast over the now cowering figure, securing it tight, and amazed everyone present by picking the whole content up like no more than a sack of potatoes—not bad for a sixty-one-year-old lifting a hefty like-aged old gent—and flinging it up onto his horse right behind the saddle.

"Better for him I don't drag it," he said, grinning, and, without another word, loped back up the snowy road out of sight.

◀▷

The day was pure golden autumn, the sky blue, and little tufts of snow glistening in the sun on all the grass clumps, rocks, and wafting off pines on slopes into the distance. Major John Brennan ("Long Neck"), riding in the lead of the contingent heading east toward Pine Ridge, was ecstatic. The charges he'd permitted to hunt returned more intact than seemed likely, and these rambunctious bucks were now submissive.

They swung along, stirrups jingling, wheels on wagons creaking.

And, lo, the spirit of Eagle Feather did speak cruelly, admonishing them for escaping from the world of all their fathers with only the skin on their backs, running away like rats. This topsy-turvy grassy ocean of the endless old herds like stars and the blades of grass and dew on the flowers of morning and the bluest skies was theirs, and their freedom to return and again know its riches needed to be grasped from the white man. And those last now-fleeing few were vexed, feeling smart the sting of shame in leaving it.

Coming to the Dakota line unmolested, the little band again stopped at the door of the plain farmhouse on what the whites called Cold Spring Creek or sometimes Stockade Beaver and the little rosy-cheeked farm girl stepped forward from her warmly-smiling parents and same-size brother to extend again to Iron Shield a cup of water, something she would always remember. He bent down from his mount and drank deeply, nodding in appreciation.

Then, he turned his horse and, kneeling quickly, laid his feathered war lance like a wreath, almost as an afterthought, down beside the weathered sign at the border in the dusting of snow. And departed from Wyoming forever.

CODA...

Still, the wonder is that the legacy of bad old thinking, shorn of the change as something unworthy, abides, bedevils, beggars, and leaves us no wiser today.

READERS GUIDE

1. Based on The Bells of Autumn, what do you think might be some of the advantages and limitations incurred by exploring historical events through fiction?

2. About half of the main characters in this novel were real people, portrayed as accurately as possible. Which were fictional? *

3. What were the major conflicts in the story and who were the primary sets of adversaries?

4. Could Old Chessler or Daniel have done anything to improve the town's attitude toward them?

5. What do you think was the basis for Martin's response to the Lakota's planned hunt?

6. To what extent do you think Martin was responsible for what happened?

7. How would you compare the various decisions made by the two sheriffs, Miller and Owens? Which would you have voted for, and why?

8. Do you think Iris would have been a good choice to manage Martin's business affairs in his absence? Why or why not?

9. What differences do you see between Newcastle in the past and in the early 20th century?

10. Describe the plight of the Lakota and its causes.

11. Do you think anything similar to what happened in this story could happen today?

12. How would you evaluate the response of the Newcastle *News-Journal*'s coverage of the events in the story?

*(Chessler, Daniel, Martin, Iris, Penny, Cammacge, Chantelle Holiday)

www.ingramcontent.com/pod-product-compliance
Lightning Source LLC
Chambersburg PA
CBHW032121020726
47494CB00007BA/2187